Some Like
It Hot

Books by K. J. Larsen

Liar, Liar
Sticks & Stones
Some Like It Hot

Some Like It Hot

A Cat DeLuca Mystery

K. J. Larsen

Poisoned Pen Press

Poisoned Pen Press
6962 E. First Ave., Ste. 103
Scottsdale, AZ 85251
www.poisonedpenpress.com
info@poisonedpenpress.com

Printed in the United States of America

To our beautiful family and friends.
You're the inspiration behind Cat DeLuca and her
outrageous family. You keep us laughing.

Acknowledgements

Our heartfelt thanks to Barbara Peters, Editor Extraordinaire; Jessica Tribble, our brilliant, blue-caped Publisher; and the amazing staff at Poisoned Pen Press.

And our love and appreciation to our sweet Papa, family, and friends. For their support, understanding and unending patience through our writing adventure.

Chapter One

When I was a kid, I knew I could fly. I cut a cape from Mama's blue silk dress and rocketed up the apple tree in our backyard. Sophie wouldn't fly with me. My chicken-shit sister hated getting dirty.

I teetered on the highest branch and threw apples at my sister. Mama ran outside screaming. "Caterina! No!"

"Jump! Jump!" Sophie sang.

"I'm flying! I'm—"

Okay. I was wrong about that.

That was the day I learned two terrible truths about my life. I can't fly.

And my sister Sophie was switched at birth.

I still climb trees and scale balconies. I peer into hotel windows and snag photos for my 8x10 glossies. Mostly I love my job. I've dodged a few bullets. And I've taken some pies in the face. I prefer chocolate.

My name is Cat DeLuca, PI. I own the Pants On Fire Detective Agency. Right now I own Bernie Martini's sorry, dumb ass.

I peered over my glass at the couple in the next booth. She was a bleach-bottle blond in a cherry red sweater that stretched tight in all the right places. Bernie was a turtleneck and sports coat guy. His fingers rubbed the tan line where his wedding band should be. The ring would be in his pocket.

I know this because I was married to a man whose ring dropped into his pocket like his finger was coated with WD-40. The cheater at the next table could be my ex. Except Johnnie Rizzo was much hotter. He was smokin' hot. He was also a lying sack of shit.

Okay, so here's the thing. My marriage to Johnnie Rizzo may have been a bust. But it taught me the low-down, sneaky ways of cheaters. And every sly, devious way to catch them.

The blond torpedoed her knockers into his chest and kissed Bernie hard. When he came up for air, his glasses dangled off his nose.

Bernie is married to my client, Olivia Martini. Yesterday, Olivia found condoms in Bernie's pocket. Two left in a four-pack. Today she's emptying their savings account and buying a condo. Tonight she'll serve up my 8x10 glossies for supper.

My flower-print purse is a camouflaged camera. I adjusted the angle to snag a shot of blondie's nimble hands beneath the table. The candy apple red finger nail polish would be a striking contrast to Bernie's khakis for the photo extravaganza.

The server delivered appetizers and drinks to the lovers' table and a lunch menu to mine. She wore gold hoops in her ears and one in her nose. She had frank, clear eyes and a decade on me. The four-leafed-clover nametag read Katie.

She rolled her eyes at Bernie and Blondie. "Ain't love grand. You know what they say."

"What? Get a room?"

Katie laughed and lowered her voice to a whisper. "Romeo is a regular. But the chick is new. I think the guy has a revolving door on his zipper, if you know what I mean. He probably has a wife with four kids trapped at home. "

I shot the love-birds a sidelong glance. Bernie hand-fed the blond a plump, buttery shrimp appetizer. When he was finished, she sucked his fingers. *Eeeeuw.*

"You think he's married?"

"Girl, I got thirteen years in this bar. I can spot the hitched ones."

I smiled. "I never would have guessed."

The pub door opened and a blast of cold air blew in a half-dozen longshoremen. They were beefy, loud, and tanked. Tierney's Irish Pub was not their first stop.

A shit-faced guy howled from the door. "Whiskey for me and my friends." His red, unfocused eyes swept the bar and settled on me. "And I'll have her."

"*Seriously?*" I said.

Katie sighed. "I should have gone to college."

She left a menu with me. "I like your flowered bag," she said over her shoulder. "It looks roomy."

I smiled. "It holds a multitude of sins."

I cut my eyes to the lovebirds playing footsie under the table. The blond laughed easily and was more fun. Bernie's perpetual dour, Eeyore-ish look had etched deep lines on his face. He resembled a Shar Pei.

Another blast of brisk air blew Santa into the bar. He was chubby and plump in his red suit, even without the stuffing. Blue eyes danced above the fluffy, white beard.

"Ho ho ho," he said.

"Hey, Nick," Shit-face shouted over the crowd. "You're uh… way early, man. What's wrong? The old lady kick ya out?"

Santa ho-ho-ho'ed his way over to the bar and spoke to a couple of guys there. The bartender checked his watch and jerked his thumb to the door that read "For Employees and Leprechauns Only." Santa nodded and disappeared through it.

I checked out the menu. Even though I was hungry, I was reluctant to order more than a light appetizer while stalking. It's the high cost of surveillance. I have to be able to leave when my mark does. Ditching an untouched meal is risky. It may as well be a neon sign for a wary cheater. An abandoned half-empty drink and some appetizers are far less suspicious.

Shouts and a loud ruckus erupted from the back of the bar. *SLAM!* A door hit the wall and the menu flew from my hands. Santa charged through the leprechaun door, black boots pounding the floor. Two muscled gangster trolls were hot on his tail.

They had guns in their coats. One waved Santa's beard in his hand.

I gazed into Santa's beardless face and Billy Bonham grinned back at me. He tweeked a thumb and pinky to his ear. "Call me."

I didn't think. I shot out a leg. The posse went tumbling over my Uggs. In a sputtering nosedive, they crashed and burned onto the backs of the tanked-up longshoremen. A drunken howl sliced the air. Chaos exploded. The fight was on.

Santa made a clean escape though the door.

I drained my glass, dropped a wad of cash on the table, and slung the camera/purse over my shoulder before scooting out the door behind Santa.

And that's how I saved Christmas.

Chapter Two

The last time I saw Bill Bonham was the year we graduated from high school. Bill was the class clown. He mooned Bridgeport from our school bus. He super-glued the principal's bum to his chair. Bill was also the smartest kid I knew. The day I told Bill I wasn't ready for an algebra test there was a mysterious explosion in his chemistry class. School was closed for two days. Bill helped me study. I aced the test.

The antics he pulled in high school didn't serve him well in college. He was expelled in his freshman year. He came home and got a job at the K.G. Brewery making Schmidt beer. Papa and Captain Bob were beat cops back then. They were partners. One night they found Billy's car parked behind the bowling alley. The windows were fogged up and the car was bouncing like a cheapo McDonald's toy.

Billy was hot and heavy in the backseat with Bob's daughter. Papa pried Bob's hands from around Bill's neck and made a deal with his partner. If Bill wasn't out of town by 10 a.m., Papa would help Bob dispose of the body. At 9:53 a.m. Bill Bonham became a soldier. Uncle Sam snagged him from Bridgeport. As far as I knew, he hadn't come back. Until now.

I darted out of Tierney's Irish Pub and scanned up and down the street. Santa was nowhere to be seen. I hotfooted across the street to the Silver Bullet, yanked my door open, and slid behind the wheel. Inga licked my ear.

"Which way did he go, girl?"

The beagle wagged her tail joyfully. Then she let out a bay and pranced her feet south toward Halsted where a vendor scooped chili on hot dogs. A different dog's howl would be all about the wienies. But I knew my partner. Inga was on the scent.

"Gotcha."

I opened my surveillance cooler and tossed her one of Tino's fat sausages. Then I whipped a U-ey and cruised south on Halsted. I caught up with Santa two blocks away. He'd ditched the red suit and was jogging incognito in reindeer boxers and black boots. I doubted he'd worked up that much of a sweat since basic training. His body was soft and his belly was a temple for Big Macs and Ding Dongs. But today Bill Bonham ran like a hunted gazelle.

I cruised to a stop and pitched the passenger door open. Santa gasped for breath.

"And what would you like for Christmas, little girl?"

"I'd like for children never to have to see Santa in his underwear again."

He dived inside and kissed my cheek. "Thanks, Cat. You saved my ass."

"Why yes, I did. Where's your car?"

"Stolen. Last week."

"Oh my God."

"Yeah. Those repo guys are jerks."

I laughed. "Same ol' Bill."

I got out and searched through my box of tricks in the trunk. Wigs, changes of clothes, jackets, a Japanese kimono—nothing for 230 pounds of junk-food junkie. I dragged a blanket from the trunk and tossed it to Bill. He pulled it around him gratefully. I slid back into the car.

"Where are you staying?" I pulled away from the curb and merged into traffic. "I'll take you home."

"With Mom—temporarily. Just until I get back on my feet. Here's the thing. She said if I come home in my underwear again, she's kicking me out."

"This has happened before?"

"Last week. Strip poker with two gorgeous women." He grinned. "Trust me, I wasn't trying to win."

"So what happened to your clothes?"

"We're playing and there's footsteps on the stoop. The red-head says, 'Shit. It's my husband.' I say, 'Husband? Shit!' And they both push me out a window. How was I supposed to know one of 'em was married?"

"You're a dog, Bill."

He winced. "I lost my wallet, money, my new Chicago Bears jacket, and my spanking new kicks."

I threw him a look. "And it didn't pop into that brain of yours they were after your new things all along?"

"What are you saying?"

"I dunno. When's the last time two gorgeous women were so hot to get you drunk and out of your clothes?"

"Shut up. It could happen."

"Uh huh."

"Women adore me. As I recall, you wanted to marry me."

"I was eight."

"You were sober."

I laughed and dragged one of Mama's cannoli from my surveillance cooler and poured coffee from my thermos while we waited at a red light. Bill wrapped his cold hands around the steaming mug.

"Their house was across the street from that creepy zombie house that scared the crap out of you on Halloween."

"And you ran all that way, naked?"

"Well, nearly." He grinned. "I've run it before."

I checked my rearview mirror. It didn't look like anyone was following us, but I made some fast twists and turns and rocketed down a few back streets to be sure.

"OK, Romeo," I said. "I'll take you home and find you something to wear."

He exaggerated a sigh. "I guess tonight one gorgeous woman will have to do."

"I guess tonight you'll make it home with your wallet."

Bill sank his teeth into the chocolate cannoli. His eyes rolled back in his head. "I've dreamt of your Mama's pastries. How's she doing anyway? Does she still grab her chest when you don't do what she wants?"

"She thinks her attacks are full blown coronaries now."

He gulped. "That sucks. I'm sorry."

"Don't be. The doctor says it's gas."

I hoisted the cooler into the backseat and wagged a finger at Inga. "Stay out of the sausages. You don't want to spoil your supper."

"You realize it's impossible to open that cooler without opposable thumbs."

"You have no idea what my partner can do."

"Hey, you're not getting nuts like your mama, are you?"

"I'm not the one in reindeer boxers and Santa boots."

"Point taken."

"Our mamas talk at church. They say you and I are their 'problem' children."

Bill gasped in mock dismay. "Not you!"

"Mama blames my profession on my wrecked marriage with Johnnie Rizzo. And she tells Father Timothy everything. He knows every humiliating event in my life."

"Really? Do share and don't leave out any of the details."

I pulled a face. "What about you. I heard you started a computer software business."

"I did. That went belly up."

"But you invented that spinning brush that sold on an infomercial."

"Not well."

"Okay. But at least you got married."

"Strike three. My wife hooked up with some loser from work. I come home one day, my clothes are on the porch, and his car is in my garage."

"Bummer."

"I hit rock bottom. It seemed everything I touched turned to shit. One night I was watching an old movie channel on cable I hijacked from a neighbor. I put a pistol to my head and pulled the trigger."

"Oh. My. God."

"The gun jammed. I couldn't even get that right." He gave a self-deprecating smile. "I guess I dozed off. When I woke, Humphrey Bogart was on the screen."

He mimicked Bogart's laconic voice. "'Such a lot of guns around town and so few brains! You know you're the second guy I've met today that seems to think a gat in the hand means the world by the tail.'"

"*The Big Sleep*," I said. "You've got a huge man-crush on Bogie."

"No. Okay, yes. But don't you get it?"

"Not even a little bit."

"That was my epiphany. At that moment I knew what I was made for."

"Oh boy."

"I was born to be a private eye. A detective. A dick. A gumshoe."

"I get it, already."

"I was born to be you. I watched every detective movie I could find on Netflix. I bought a trench coat. Took an online investigator's course. I came home and opened a little hole-in-the-wall office in Bridgeport."

"You're a real Philip Marlowe."

He slipped into Bogie again. "'Okay, Marlowe' I said to myself. 'You're a tough guy. You've been sapped twice, choked, beaten silly with a gun, shot in the arm until you're crazy as a couple of waltzing mice. Now let's see you do something really tough—'"

I groaned.

"Do you want to hear more Bogie?"

"What I'd like is for you to put your pants on. And I want to know what happened back there."

"Okay. Here I am, working my first big case. I'm undercover. In disguise. Chapter fourteen in the correspondence course."

"You could've been killed."

He flashed his disarming smile. "But I wasn't. You were there. It's a sign. We should go into business together."

"I have a partner."

"But *I* can open a cooler."

"The job is filled. Back off. Just out of curiosity, do you have a license?"

"License—shmicense. Okay, so technically my 'Private Detective License Packet' has not been completed." He did the air quotes with his fingers for added emphasis. "But I am really close. I only have forty hours of firearm training to do. Then one or two minor, technical hoops to jump through. But then I will be completely above board.

An unexpected feeling of dread twisted my gut. For one curious moment I couldn't breathe. Now *that* was a sign. A big fat flashing neon sign. No way were things going to turn out well.

I massaged my temples. "Those thugs were carrying some serious hardware, Billy. Why were they chasing you?"

"I didn't wait around for them to explain."

"You must have some idea."

"Not really."

"Make a wild guess. What did they want?"

"Well, if I was a betting man…"

"You are."

He stuffed the last bite of cannoli in his mouth. "I'd say they wanted to kill me."

"And they say *I* piss people off."

Chapter Three

My house in Bridgeport is a brick bungalow on a corner lot with a big front porch and a swing. A separate entrance on the side of the house opens to my office. It's for clients. The cheatees. I buy my tissues by the case at Costco. Of course, not all clients are horribly wounded. Some are relieved to end a bad relationship. Some use my 8x10 glossies to maximize their financial settlement. Some want to save their marriages. Some post my 8x10 glossies on Facebook, MySpace, or even make a video montage for YouTube with their favorite song. And sometimes, someone like Cleo peppers her husband's lying, cheating ass with buckshot.

Cleo Jones is a former client-turned-assistant for the Pants On Fire Detective Agency. She's fiercely loyal and her enthusiasm is unparalleled. As is her disturbing eagerness to shoot people.

I pulled in front of my house and parked behind Cleo's canary-yellow Corvette.

The Corvette had belonged to Cleo's no-good husband, Walter. Cleo recently acquired Walter's worldly possessions when somebody put a bullet in his chest. Walter had a knack for pissing people off. He pissed off Cleo when he ran off with her sister, her dog, and all her money. But Cleo didn't kill Walter. Someone else beat her to it.

"That's my assistant's car," I said. "Cleo's oven is on the fritz. She's borrowing mine."

He grinned. "I hope she likes your new partner."

Inga growled from the backseat.

"Cleo is catering the appetizers for Mama's Bridge Club, and she's trying out some recipes. It's at Mrs. Millani's house. Mama recommended Cleo, and she wants everything to be perfect."

"I hope she makes buffalo wings."

"No way. Mama wants to wow Mrs. Millani."

"You can't get more wow than buffalo wings."

"You are such a guy."

I killed the engine and checked the street. The coast was clear.

"Pull that blanket around you, and we'll make a dash for the front door."

Bill slid out of the car and hitched the blanket tight. It was short and barely closed around his Hostess-anointed frame. White calves showed bare above black Santa boots. He looked like a flasher.

Mrs. Pickins, the neighborhood snoop, appeared from nowhere.

"Get her, Inga," I whispered. Inga wagged her tail.

Mrs. Pickins screeched, "That man has no pants! He's a pervert. Hot Pants Detective Agency indeed!"

I felt Bill smile behind me.

I gritted my teeth and whispered. "Flash your reindeer and I'll dress you in pink."

I scooted up the steps, unlocked the door, and shoved Bill and Inga inside.

"You break your mama's heart, Caterina De—"

I kicked the door shut behind me. "Tell me something I don't know."

I took Bill's blanket and folded it. "You can take a hot shower while I find you something to wear."

Beau, Cleo's black Tibetan Terrier, came rocketing to the door, sounding the alarm. Cleo trailed after, her apron dusted with flour.

"We have company," Cleo said.

"This is Bill," I said.

"Indeed." She checked out the reindeer boxer guy and smiled. "I like the soft tufts of hair around his man boobs."

"You do?" I said.

"Ho ho ho," Bill winked. "You like Rudolph?"

"Keep his nose in the barn," I said.

I heard a gasp behind Cleo. I shuddered. I'd know that whimper anywhere. It's the sound Mama makes when her daughter's going to hell and she's dialing her priest. Mama has Father Timothy on speed dial.

Unfortunately, she wasn't alone. Mama and Mrs. Millani gaped at the near-naked man in my hallway. Mama gripped her heart. Mrs. Millani dragged a wide-eyed gaze from Rudolph. She touched Mama's sleeve. "Are you alright, dear?"

Mama wasn't alright at all. Her eyes were horrified. Her cheeks were hot. She was mortified.

I glared at my assistant. Cleo shrugged.

"What? I said we had company."

A faint wheezing escaped Mama's lips. Margaret Millani is the one woman I've seen Mama want to impress. She and her husband Ken are the only millionaires Mama knows.

I sucked in a breath. "Call 911," I said. "Somebody mugged Santa Claus."

◇◇◇

The tale I told of Santa's suit-snatching assault would crack the heart of Scrooge. At least Mrs. Millani was moved. Mama didn't believe my story for a minute, but later she thanked me and told me to go to Confession.

The women fussed over Bill and wrapped a down quilt around him. Mrs. Millani made hot chocolate. Cleo tossed in rum. Mama fed Bill a fat plate of appetizers. There weren't any chicken wings. Instead we had Garlicky Doused Shrimp, a Tomato Parmesan Tart, a Carmelized-Onion and Gorgonzola Grilled Pizza, Chicken and Sun-dried Tomato Bruschetta, and Raspberry Tiramisu.

Bill's eyes went glassy. "Wow," he said.

I found guy clothes in the guestroom closet. My brother, Rocco, stayed with me last summer when someone dumped a dead rat in my bed. I selected a soccer uniform that said *Coach* on the front of the jacket. *Rocco DeLuca* was embossed on back. The getup was roomy on Rocco. Bill tugged, squeezed, and finally managed to compress himself into it.

Mrs. Millani drove Mama home before Chicago's finest, in the form of my cousin Frankie, answered the 911. Mrs. Pickens ogled from her front window. I saw her self-satisfied smirk below binoculars as Frankie's squad car came roaring up the street, sirens at full scream. The tires screeched their complaint as he slid to a stop at the curb.

Frankie DeLuca spent the first twenty years of his life preparing to be a G-man. He became an excellent marksman. At fourteen, he shot an unsuspecting neighbor's donut hole from his own kitchen window. At fifteen, he wire-tapped the school cheerleaders' phones. His mistake was not studying for the psych eval. When he was turned down by the FBI for general insanity, he launched a promising career with the Chicago PD. My crazy cousin was just what they were looking for.

I opened the door before Frankie beat it down. He charged inside, gun drawn. Frankie stiffened and his gaze narrowed on the guy sipping cocoa on the couch.

"Is this the perpetrator?"

"Put the gun away, Frankie," I said. "It was a false alarm."

Frankie's face crashed. He'd like to knock off a few rounds to impress Cleo.

Cleo and Frankie have a "thing." I warned my assistant not to date my crazy cousin Frankie. Maybe because I have a rule against dating psycho men. They're unpredictable. I don't know what my cousin Frankie would do if he was pissed off. But I know what Cleo does. She hauls out the buckshot and fires.

"Hi, Frank," Bill said.

"You remember Bill Bonham," I said. "He recently moved back to Bridgeport."

Billy grunted. "I'm a private dick now. Like Cat. We're working a few cases together."

"Excuse me?" Cleo demanded more than questioned.

"You want in, Frank?" Bill said.

"*No!*" I said.

"Bonham?" Frankie reluctantly holstered his weapon. "I thought Captain Bob shot you."

He sounded disappointed.

"Nah. I ran faster."

Frankie's gaze took in the coaching uniform stretched tight over Bill's ample, Santa-like gut. "You don't look so fast."

"He can still jet," I said. "I've seen it with my own eyes."

Chapter Four

Bill and Cleo hung out at the house, and I wrapped up the Martini case. I printed the photographs and delivered Olivia's 8x10 glossies. Olivia Martini didn't need me to tell her Bernie was a putz. While Bernie was at the pub getting his glasses steamed, she hired a brutal divorce lawyer. And she made an offer on a condo near her sister's house in Glen Ellyn. Olivia Martini was going to be okay.

I buzzed home and met a pizza delivery guy on my front porch. The door was open. Green Day blasted from my speakers. And Bill Bonham rummaged through the pockets of his borrowed sweats. He came up with lint.

I settled with the pizza guy and carried the pie to the living room. The furniture had been shoved aside, and Billy and Cleo were dancing to the Red Hot Chili Peppers. They'd made a sizeable dent in a pitcher of margaritas. If I acted fast, I could squeeze another glass out of it.

Bill caught my hand and spun me around. When we were kids, I was taller than he was. I still was.

"They played this song at graduation. Remember? You were dating that dumb jock back then."

"Dumb? The guy was a Greek god. He went to the University of Michigan on a football scholarship."

Bill snorted. "If he graduated, someone did his homework for him. I tutored him in Chemistry. The elevator didn't reach the top floor."

"I was young. If I had cared about the top floor I wouldn't

have married Johnnie Rizzo! I remember you were hot and heavy with Captain Bob's daughter."

"I was crazy about that girl."

"I happen to know she's available. Call her."

"You think her dad would still shoot me?"

"I'm pretty sure he would. If anything, you proved one thing today."

"Yeah?"

"You can still run."

Bill dipped me low, lingering above me a long moment. I thought Cleo would appreciate the view of his man-breasts.

"Maybe I'll call her *after* we find the ice earrings. But I won't go bragging about my windfall. I made *that* mistake with my ex-wife. She's stalking me like she wants to get back together. She wants that diamond for herself and her new boy toy."

"Hold up here, Studmuffin. After *we* find *what?*"

"Haven't you been paying attention? You may have more experience, but if we're going to work together, you've got to focus." He did that annoying gesture, darting two fingers back and forth between our eyes.

I wriggled my way back up to my feet and kicked his shin. "Diamond earrings? *Seriously?* Is that why those thugs were chasing you?"

"I *may*, I repeat *may*, have been looking for a safe in the brick wall. But they couldn't tell what I was doing. Not when you think about it."

"They couldn't tell?" I heard my voice rise to a pitch I'd only heard from Mama. "They chased you out like a dog. They knew exactly what you were doing. And another thing, what the hell do you know about cracking safes, anyway?"

"Safe cracking 101. It was chapter twelve in my correspondence course."

I grabbed my hair. "Awwggh!"

Cleo shimmied around the room, purring "Wake Me Up When September Ends" in her vibrant voice.

I grabbed the margarita pitcher. "We're taking this pizza party to the kitchen table. Santa has a lot of explaining to do."

◇◇◇

Bill recounted his story, lapsing from time to time into Bogie's voice. I clamped my mouth, gritted my teeth, and listened.

"I got this client named Cristina McTigue. So, four years ago, she's workin' as a bartender at Tierney's Irish Pub. One night she locks up and forgets her purse. She drives back to the pub. Lets herself in. Her boss' car is parked outside, and she wanders back to talk about a shift change."

Cleo said, "Did she get her purse back?"

"Ya, I guess."

"Cuz I hate to lose a purse."

"I'm guessing this isn't a story about the bartender's purse," I said.

Cleo kicked her chair back and dragged three beers from the fridge. "Just sayin'."

"The thing is, there's this other guy with the boss," Bill said. "The guy's dangling these killer diamond earrings in the air. I mean, the chandelier kind. Lots of ice. Tierney says, 'I'll take those diamonds now.' The guy says, 'Screw you.' And Boom! The boss pulls a gun and shoots him dead. Cool as ice."

Cleo nodded, "I've had my share of jerk bosses."

I threw her a look.

Bill took a long pull from his bottle and said, "Cristina sees Tierney take the earrings out of the dead guy's hand. He drops them in a wall safe with some papers and fat stacks of money. He turns around, and there's Cristina. Eyes wide as saucers. She runs. The chase is on."

Cleo grunted. "The girl's got some serious angels to be tellin' this story."

"No shit. Two cops are cruising by. They hear the gunshot, come bustin' through the door. Cristina escapes out back. She races home, drags her daughter from her bed, and drives west until she runs out of road and hits the ocean."

"Why run?" I said. "Why not go to the police?"

Billy did a palms-up. "She says Tierney has connections. She's scared of him."

"I don't run for no man," Cleo said. "I'd fill his bum with buckshot."

I pulled another slice from the box. "I remember the case. Tierney went to prison."

"He did four years. He was released last month. Had some time shaved off for good behavior." Billy said.

Cleo snorted. "That's a load of crap."

"The economy sucks and prisons are overcrowded." Billy shrugged.

I shook peppers on my cheese. "I don't remember anything in the papers about diamond earrings."

"As far as we know, only three people knew about the ice. Kyle Tierney, Cristina, and the dead guy. He's not talking."

"If your client's so frightened of Tierney, what's she doing back in Bridgeport?"

"She wants to blackmail him," Cleo said. "I know I would."

"Not smart," I said.

"Cristina hired me to break into the safe and take the earrings, of course. If the rocks aren't there, she says the cash will do."

"Jeeze, Bill. What the hell are you thinking?"

He grinned. "It's not theft, really."

"No. It really is."

"I gotta go with Bill on this one," Cleo said.

"Cristina doesn't care about the money," Bill said. "She's not like that."

"Uh huh."

"She has a brain tumor. She's dying. It's the only reason she came back."

"Poor thing." Cleo sighed and chugged down her beer.

I pressed my fingers to my eyeballs. Bill was a runaway train. And Cleo was his big, fat caboose.

Bill poked his head in the fridge and came out with more beer. "Cristina is sick. She doesn't have insurance. She wants financial security for Halah, her fifteen-year-old daughter."

"Hear, hear," Cleo said.

"When Cristina's boss killed that guy, she lost everything too. She had plans to go back to school."

I said, "Cristina needs a lawyer. Not a private dick. She needs to sue the guy."

"She may not have time."

"Okay, I get it," I said. "But breaking into a tough guy's safe isn't like super-gluing the principal's desk to his office ceiling."

"Bill did that?" Cleo said with admiration.

"Don't encourage him," I said.

"It was Cristina's idea to dress up like Santa. I went in during a shift change. I told the bartender I was there to talk about a Christmas event. Cristina knew he'd tell me to wait in back. No one wants to see Santa on a bar stool."

"Or a priest in a whore house," Cleo said.

"So I'm in the back room looking for the safe. My hands are all over the wall when a dude walks in. I say, 'Ho, ho ho. Where's that damn chimney?'"

"Smooth," Cleo said.

"The guy's a prick. He's got no Christmas spirit. He lunges at me, so I ran."

I squeezed Bill's hand. "Isn't it possible Cristina is confused? She may not know what she's talking about."

His spine stiffened.

"Listen. I had a concussion last summer. I know what it's like when everyone thinks you see dead people. Mama couldn't look at me without crossing herself. So I say this with all compassion for your client."

"Say what?"

"Cristina may not remember the events as they occurred."

"What are you suggesting?"

"Nut job," Cleo sang.

I kicked her under the table. "Your client has a brain tumor. The safe. The diamonds. It's possible she imagined them."

Bill chucked a fist to his chest like Mama and choked.

"Hey, Bill. I'm just saying."

"Stop. You're giving me gas.

Chapter Five

We finished off every slice of pizza in the box. And the bottle of tequila, another casualty of the night. A pint of Ben & Jerry's was next to fall. We polished off a pot of strong coffee and I drove Bill home.

His phone blared "The Death March." He made a face. "It's my soon-to-be-ex."

I swallowed a smile. "Aren't you going to answer?"

He dragged out the cell. "Go to hell," he said and dropped it back in his pocket.

"At least you're not bitter," I said.

"I'm a dumb ass for marrying her. I want Cleo to shoot her."

"Sorry. She used all her buckshot on Walter."

The tequila was totally messing with his vibe. "Uh huh. Well at least my wife can't bother me here. She's far away in a foreign country."

"Where were you living?"

"Kansas. There's a direct flight to Oz. What about you, Cat? Are you seeing anybody?"

Until recently, I would have said no. After my divorce, I had a long dry spell in the dating department. The only naked men I saw were through the lens of my camera. It wasn't pretty.

When you're in the business of catching cheaters, you're exposed to more hairy backsides than any woman should have to see. Sometimes you see things you really wish you hadn't. On a bad day, you could go blind.

"I'm dating Chance Savino. He's a good guy. He works for the FBI."

Bill chuckled. "Your family's gotta love that. Everyone knows the DeLucas hate the FBI."

"Yeah. For turning down my crazy cousin Frankie. But Mama hates the tick-tock of my biological clock more. I'm thirty. It keeps her awake at night."

"Your mama likes this Savino?"

"She'll embrace any man who's reasonably sober, has a decent sperm count, and has insurance."

"I got one out of three."

I laughed. "Enough about Rudolph."

I pulled to the curb in front of Billy's mama's house. A cocker spaniel barked in the window. A rerun of *Murder She Wrote* played on TV.

"Thanks for everything," he said. "The ride, the pizza, and this really sweet coaching uniform. I'll add it to the repertoire of my very own soon-to-be disguise box. "

"I'd like to meet your client."

"*Our* client, partner."

"I'll come by your office in the morning and meet your client. We'll do lunch."

"My office is a little hole in the wall on the south end. Next to Olga's Swedish Massage."

"That place gets raided all the time."

"Not for almost four days." He grinned. "It's just until I get set up and a good clientele rolling through here. Then I'll look for better digs. But look at that." He nudged me with his elbow. "We're on the same wavelength. I'm meeting Cristina at Taqueria La Mexicana at eleven. I'll introduce you then."

"Eleven. Taqueria La Mexicana."

He stepped out of the car and poked his head in the door. He gave a crooked smile. "You'll always be the one that got away, Cat."

I blew him a kiss. "We were eight, Bill.

After dropping Bill off at his mom's door, I cruised by Tino's on my way home. Tino is a round bear of a man with a secret 007 past and a mysterious present. He usually knows what goes down in Bridgeport before the cops do. He's the go-to man for information.

The deli was closed, but the lights were on. Max's Hummer was parked in front.

I bypassed the closed sign and scooted inside. The wonderful aromas of giardinera and fresh pasta filled my senses. Tino's is like being in Mama's kitchen, but with more wine and less guilt.

I found Max and Tino hunched over a chess board.

"Caterina! Come. Sit. Tell us about your day." Tino's boisterous voice filled the room.

"Hi, guys. Whatcha doin'? Spy stuff? War games? Taking over the world?"

"Such a wild imagination you have, my sweet. We speak of sausages here."

"Uh huh." I winked.

Max leaned back in his chair, with hands laced behind his head. His body was long and lean with the kind of chiseled muscle definition that had been reproduced by sculptors' hands for centuries. And I was one woman who was eternally grateful.

"Today was an exciting day in Bridgeport," Max said.

"You're changing the subject."

"I am." Max's golden brown eyes sparkled. "Santa Claus was spotted in Bridgeport today."

"Really?" I said. "How about that."

"Kyle Tierney's guys came around asking about him. And his accomplice."

"Let me guess. About three feet tall, wearing funny shoes?"

"You would go straight for the shoes for identification."

"And, your point is…?" I winked at Tino.

"As I was saying…" Max waited for Tino to stop chuckling. "…Santa was at the Irish Pub, ran out the door, ditched his Santa suit and ran down the streets of Bridgeport. Naked."

"Bet that wasn't pretty," I said.

"It wasn't," Max said. "I wouldn't mind seeing his elf naked, though."

I frowned, "Elves are notoriously frumpy."

"This one wasn't. Five nine or ten. Long, chestnut hair. The kind of dreamy green eyes men go to battle for."

"Tierney's men said this?"

Max winked. "I may have embellished a little."

"I am not the only woman in Bridgeport who has green eyes and brown hair." I grabbed a clump of my hair and shook it at him for emphasis.

Max took a breath. "The waitress said Santa's assistant had a huge flowered purse."

"That's it?" I whipped out my Dr. Pepper Lip Smacker from my flowered bag and coated it on my lips. "Circumstantial evidence at best."

When I lie, my lips itch. It's my tell. Ever since I was eleven I have been addicted to that little maroon Lip Smacker tube.

"The waitress said the elf spent the whole time staring at some schmuck cheating on his wife." Max did a palms up. "Santa's elf and a Hootchie stalker? This woman obviously has mad skills."

"You don't know the half of my mad skills," I smiled conspiratorially.

"I am always willing to learn. Anytime, day or night." Max looked deep into my eyes.

I blushed profusely and jumped a foot into the air when the timer buzzed in the kitchen.

Tino pulled a tray of bruschetta from the oven. Max selected a bottle of Chianti from the wine rack while I grabbed plates and glasses.

"So who is this Santa?" Tino said.

"Billy Bonham."

"Ahhh, I heard he was back in town."

"Of course you did."

"Billy went to school with Cat," Tino said for Max's benefit. "Smart kid. Reminded me of myself."

Max grinned. "Because he was so smart?"

"Because he spent so much time in the principal's office. Captain Bob chased him out of town a decade ago."

"What did he do?"

"He got too friendly with the Captain's daughter."

Max laughed. "I thought you said he was smart."

I poured the wine. "If men were smart when it comes to women, I wouldn't have enough clients to buy Inga's sausages."

"When it comes to women, men are weak," Tino said philosophically. "Cat has the sausages and photographs to prove it."

"What does Billy do?"

"He's a private dick. He's watched too many old movies. He thinks he's the modern day Humphrey Bogart."

"Sam Spade," Max said. "Now that was a tough guy."

"I'm working a case with him. His client was a bartender at Tierney's when that guy was killed four years ago. She says she saw her boss pull the trigger. A deliberate, cold blooded homicide."

Tino's brow shot up. "That's not how it played out in court, and I never heard any different."

I recapped what Billy told me about the bartender, Cristina. It was harder to swallow without the tequila.

"Let me understand," Tino said. "Billy's client returns to Chicago, and hires the least qualified, least experienced investigator in Bridgeport, if not all of Chicago. And she signs up this guy? Something is not kosher."

"He's a Sam Spade wannabe," Max said. "I know women. They love that macho bravado."

I shrugged, "Billy's client thinks Tierney owes her. She's here to collect."

"Maybe a dozen private dicks turned her down already," Tino said. "This Billy lacked the experience—and the good sense—to do the same."

"She told Billy she chose him because he was new in town. She figured if he didn't know Tierney, he wouldn't be tempted to sell her out."

"And the Santa gig?"

"It was a ploy to get into Tierney's back room and find a hidden safe."

"What a dumb shit idea," Max critiqued.

"What can I say? Billy took an online detective course. He knows just enough to be dangerous to himself."

"Billy Bonham will be a good detective someday," Tino said. "He just has to get the knack of it."

"Maybe, if he lives that long," Max said. "I hear he's a fast runner."

"What do you remember about the guy who died at the pub four years ago?" I said.

Tino stroked his double chin. "Name was Mitchell, I believe. I'll ask around. Let you know what I learn."

Taking the last swallow of my Chianti, I snagged a bruschetta to go and kissed Tino on the cheek. "Thanks, Tino."

"Hey, you forgot my kiss." Max tried to grab my arm but I scooted to the door.

I smiled and winked. "No, I didn't."

◇◇◇

The phone blared beside my bed, jolting me from own "Boulevard of Broken Dreams." My words slurred with sleep.

"Pants On Fire Detective Agency. We catch liars and cheats."

The voice was grave. "Cat."

"Rocco?"

I squinted at the clock. 2:07.

"Why is your old boyfriend wearing my coaching uniform?" my brother said.

"You're not seriously waking me to ask that question."

"Just answer me, Cat."

There was intensity behind his words. And something else I didn't immediately identify. Anguish. The foreboding that twisted my gut earlier was back with a vengeance.

"Why?"

The question was a lie. I didn't want to know. I wanted to crawl under my covers and return to dreamland.

"Bill Bonham was walking his mother's dog around one this morning," Rocco said. "There was a shooting."

Billy? The fear in my gut intensified, piercing at my chest and knotting my throat.

"I'm sorry, Cat. I was called in because the victim was wearing my jacket. It's too early to tell, but it may be a random drive-by."

I rocked on my bed, unable to speak.

"Cat?"

When my words came, a sob carried them. "Somebody killed my Santa."

Chapter Six

I sat in Billy's hole-in-the-wall office and stared at the Philip Marlowe trench-coat hanging by the door. I wasn't entirely sure how Inga and I got there. I didn't remember firing up the Silver Bullet. Or finding Billy's detective agency with the poster of Bogie on the door. I was somewhat surprised, and relieved, that I wasn't still wearing my Betty Boop night shirt.

I studied a crumpled receipt tossed on Billy's desk. It was dated yesterday morning. Billy's last breakfast was an omelet at Belle's Cafe. I hoped it was a really good one. There were three omelets on the ticket. The bartender and her daughter ate with him.

I wasn't the first person that night to let myself in uninvited. The office had been tossed when I arrived. Drawers were dumped. Papers and files strewn everywhere.

I picked up the mess and thumbed through files. Billy had picked up a few clients in his short career. A guy seeking an old girlfriend. An adoptee looking for her birth parents. A woman in a bitter custody battle over a Bichon Frisé named Coochie.

One case file was pointedly missing: Cristina McTigue, bartender and witness to a grisly murder.

Max and Tino said Tierney's goons came sniffing around looking for Billy. Well, they found him, all right. Tierney got the file and he got Billy. Now he had everything he needed to silence the bartender.

I had to find Cristina before he did. I closed my eyes and replayed everything Billy told me about his case. I went over it and over it again and again until I must have fallen asleep. I was jarred awake by jabbing fingers. Or maybe it was the guy's bad breath.

I pushed him away. "Step back. You're in my bubble."

He had graying, sleeked back hair and bushy black brows. I knew who he was. He had dollar signs for eyes.

He was the landlord.

"Where's Billy?"

"I'm Cat DeLuca, Billy's partner."

"Billy didn't tell me he had a partner."

"He's the strong, silent type."

"I'm Davis. I own this dump. Bonham is two weeks overdue. I'm here to collect."

"I expect Billy paid first and last month?"

"What of it."

"Last month was his first. This month is his last. I'll have the office cleaned out before the end of the month."

"The lease requires a thirty day notice."

"Take it out of the deposit."

I jotted my name on a scrap of paper and handed it to him. "Call me if you need anything else. I'm taking care of things from now on."

I kicked my chair back and nudged him to the door.

He sputtered, all pissy. "Bonham owes me two more week's rent. I'll collect."

"Good luck with that."

I looked around for my cell and decided I left it in the car. I used Billy's phone to make a call.

"I'm sorry about Billy," Uncle Joey said. "We'll get the guy who did this."

"It was Kyle Tierney. I'm sure of it."

"Have you talked to Captain Bob?"

"I'm heading there now. I'm hoping you can pull some strings for me."

"I'm a frickin' puppeteer."

"The murder at the Irish Pub four years ago. I'd like to see the photos and evidence collected at the crime scene."

"The boxes are sealed and gathering dust in the evidence room."

"Is that a problem?"

"I got a guy on the inside. He'll give me anything I want for a good bottle of Scotch and two tickets to a Bears game."

"Thanks. Let me know what I owe you."

"I got it covered. An assistant coach owes me. I made some messy charges go away."

"And the booze?"

Uncle Joey laughed. "I got a case of Blue Label Johnny Walker at home. Fell off the back of a truck."

I smiled. I didn't even want to know how he got the Ferrari.

Chapter Seven

I was at the door of the Ninth Precinct, chomping on a bear claw, when Captain Bob showed up to work. I knew he wouldn't be glad to see me. He's been known to slam the door in my face. So I softened the blow with two coffees and a bag of donuts. I've never seen him turn down a lemon crème.

Bob groaned when he saw me. His eyes were a sleep-deprived red. He looked as bad as I did.

"Caterina DeLuca."

I waggled the white bakery sack.

"Are there lemon-crèmes in that bag?" he asked.

"You know it."

He reached for the bag, and I held on tight.

"I come with the donuts."

"Dammit."

I gave up the bag and trotted behind Captain Bob to his office.

"I know why you're here. I'm sorry about Bonham." He said it almost like he meant it. "I know you were close."

"We were engaged once," I said soberly.

He blinked. "I didn't know."

"People loved Bill."

"Maybe people who don't have daughters."

He moved around the desk and dropped hard on his chair. I sat down and set my coffee on his desk.

"I was with Bill yesterday."

"Of course you were."

"What is that supposed to mean?"

"People die around you, Caterina. If I were superstitious, I'd run like hell."

"It's not my fault. It's not like I kill them."

"It's not like you bring them luck. When I hear there's a homicide in Bridgeport, I look around for you."

"That hurts, Bob. I'm here to help you arrest the man who killed Billy Bonham."

He took a bite out of his donut. "How do you know he wasn't in the wrong place at the wrong time? I'm leaning toward a random shooting."

"The shooting wasn't random. It was a deliberate attack on Santa Claus."

"The Irish Pub?" Captain Bob smacked a palm on his head. "I should've known it was Bonham. He can piss off the wrong people almost as good as you. No wonder he's dead."

"Thanks a lot."

"Witnesses saw a man in a Santa suit running from Tierney's Pub. He was stripping layers of red and white as he ran."

"I didn't know someone reported it."

"People report naked men. 911 lines light up. It's not pretty."

Bob grunted. "It was all over the radio. Do you know what it's like to have to tell your grandkids that Santa's a perv?"

"Poor Billy. He finally got his fifteen minutes of fame and he missed it."

"I'm sorry it didn't work out between you two. Believe me, you're better off without him. He's just another loser who broke your heart."

"Why do you assume *he* dumped *me*?"

"You haven't had the best luck with men. Nothing's kept a secret for long in Bridgeport."

"Yeah." Thanks to Mama.

"The guy had problems. He was reported sneaking around the neighborhood wearing a sock and his skivvies."

"Billy wasn't streaking. He sucks at strip poker."

"Another hand or two and I'd have had to arrest him."

I slammed my hands down, leaning over the desk. "Arrest Kyle Tierney."

He stuck his face in the donut bag. "You got a Bavarian cream in here?"

"Dammit, Bob, I've got your killer. I'm a trained investigator."

Bob belted a laugh and choked on his donut. "If you're investigating Tierney, it's because his wife has her panties in a twist."

"That's cold, Bob. Billy knew something about the pub murder that could cause big trouble for Tierney."

"You'll forgive me for being skeptical."

"There was a witness. A bartender. She saw her boss pull the trigger. If Tierney killed Billy to silence him, he'll go after the bartender next."

"Tierney's done his time. Besides, there were no witnesses. Both the FBI and the Chicago PD were unable to come up with one. But you're telling me one of Bridgeport's most incompetent, unscrupulous screw-ups did."

"Bill was a private detective. He had the trench coat to prove it."

He rummaged in a drawer and dragged out a roll of antacids. "What was he doing in that Santa suit? He was obviously up to no good."

I thought about Bill's botched burglary. "You don't know that."

Bob cocked a brow. "When you were five, you said your baby sister was dropped off by gypsies. You still can't lie worth a damn."

"That thing I said about Sophie is true."

Bob came around the desk, scooted me off my chair and nudged me to the door. "Your dad and I go way back."

"He helped you chase Billy out of town when you caught him with your daughter."

"Actually he kept me from killing him." He popped a Tums in his mouth. "I'll have a couple guys check out your story."

"Thanks, Bob. You came through for me."
"I said that to get you out of my office."
He slammed the door in my face.

Chapter Eight

I cruised across Bridgeport toward Belle's Café. I knew Billy ate his last omelet there yesterday morning. There were three omelets on the rumpled ticket I found. Two coffees and one hot chocolate. The hot chocolate would go to Halah, Cristina's fifteen-year-old daughter. Cocoa is nice. But coffee is a lifeline. I was betting Billy's client ate breakfast close to her hotel. And if she didn't know Bill was gone, she could be at Belle's now. Or at one of the hotels nearby. I had to find her before her psycho boss did.

I took a quick detour that would take me by Tierney's Irish Pub. When we were kids, Grandpa DeLuca told stories about this once tough Chicago neighborhood, back when rich mobsters were local heroes and people went missing in the night. Bridgeport has softened since then. The meat-packing district has been converted to trendy restaurants and apartments. But as far as I was concerned, at least one monster remained.

I drove past the pub slowly while squinting in the window. It was too early for lunch. On my third sweep by, I snagged a parking spot across the street and dragged out the binoculars. Bill's killer sat smugly at a window table with two suits and a pile of papers. Tierney's skin was still a pasty prison white. But he'd resumed his life where he left it in handcuffs four years ago. Hardly missed a beat.

I thought of Billy laid out on the coroner's slab. My heart hurt. I rubbed my eyes to squelch the image. It didn't go away.

I zoomed my spy eyes on Tierney's Varvatos suit and soft blue silk shirt. There was a platter of sweet breads, three coffees, and a bottle of Jameson Whiskey on the table. The anger swelled in me. Bitter and toxic.

And then it happened. There was an unexpected and decided disconnect between my feet and my head. Because my head was telling me to stay in the car, but my feet kicked the car door and stomped across the street. They tramped through the door and past the beefy guy who'd snagged Santa's beard. His blackened eye twitched when he saw me. I counted the knuckles on his bruised cheek.

I'd say the longshoremen won that round.

"Wussy," I snickered. My feet clomped to the boss' table.

I felt Tierney's raw energy before his lecherous gaze traveled a long, slow line from my shoes to my murderous green eyes. I felt my fingers twitch. He had to know I'd cheerfully wring his neck.

"We open at eleven." He smiled. "Unless you're here for the dancing job."

I resisted the urge to feed him a sandwich de knuckle. "Bill Bonham was my friend."

"Bill Bonham." He rubbed his chin. "That name, it was on the radio this morning. I don't remember why."

"Because he's dead," I spat out at him.

"I'm sorry for your loss."

"Why did you kill him?"

He snorted. "What are you talking about? I hadn't heard his name until this morning."

"Here's a name for you. Santa."

"This Bonham was the phantom Santa?" No attempt at surprise there. "If what you say is true, why should I kill him?"

"Because Billy knew the truth about what happened here four years ago."

The ice-gray eyes pierced a chill through me. "Get out."

"You're going down, Kyle Tierney. It maybe not be today. But someday soon."

I said it like Bogie. I did it for Billy.

Tierney returned his gaze to the suits at his table. I was dismissed.

I picked up his glass of one-hundred-dollar-a-bottle whiskey and dumped it over his head. I swear I heard Billy laugh.

The bartender came running with a towel. Tierney spit words through gritted teeth.

"Grief has clouded your judgment. I won't see you in here again."

The beefy guy who snagged Santa's wig muscled his way over to me. He was huge. I realized, too late, that it took four hunky longshoremen to make him look wussy. I figured it was too late to take that back.

In one swift motion, he slung me over his shoulder, retraced my steps, and stalked out the door. A blast of cold, lake wind hit my face.

I kicked my feet and pummeled his back with my fists. "Put me down, you big-fat-piece-of-crap."

The cock of a pistol clicked in beefy boy's ear. "FBI, asshole. You heard the lady."

I knew that voice. It cheered me considerably.

The guy dropped me, none too gingerly, to my feet. "This woman was harassing the customers. I removed her from the premises because she refused to leave on her own." He shrugged. "Besides, she's a pain in the ass."

"Is that true?" Chance Savino said.

I kicked beefy guy hard in the shin. "Shoot this man!"

Chance smiled. "I'd say you're even."

I wrestled a hand in my bag and pulled out a taser. *Zzzzzzzz.*

Beefy guy dropped to his knees and groaned.

"*Now* we're even," I said.

"Police brutality."

I dropped the stun gun in my bag. "Hey. I'm just a concerned citizen."

"She's freakin' crazy!"

"Now *that* hurt my feelings," I said

Savino twisted the guy's collar and jerked him to his feet.

Chance Savino is six-feet-two of gorgeous hotness. He released the collar and beefy guy bolted into the pub. Savino chuckled and hooked an arm around my shoulder. We walked across the street to my car.

"What the hell are you doing here, Cat?"

"I'm a detective, dammit. I was gathering evidence."

The cobalt blues smiled.

"What are *you* doing here?" I countered. "Aren't you testifying in that kidnapping case today?"

"On my way. Rocco told me about Bonham. And you weren't answering your phone. I wanted to be sure you're okay."

"My brother's a big fat tattletale."

Actually, Rocco is my best friend. Except when he's bossy. He forgets I'm a big girl now, and I don't need him to come running every time I do something stupid.

"Rocco was afraid you'd do something crazy."

"Crazy?" I shoved him.

"Like going after Kyle Tierney. You can't take him down with great legs and a taser."

"Ha! I have a gun." I reached behind my back and whipped out my Dr. Pepper Lip Smacker. I winced. My 9mm was in a drawer at home, keeping all of Victoria's Secrets safe.

"Oops."

Chance shook his head. "You brought lipstick to a gun fight."

I smeared Dr. Pepper on my lips. "You didn't need to come, Savino. I had it handled."

"I saw you handling the muscle when I arrived."

"I like to be on top."

Chance smiled and our eyes held a moment. Then he pulled up his sleeve and checked his watch. It was a Mickey Mouse Rolex. A gift from his parents. Savino's parents are ex-hippies and tree-hugging vegetarians. They belong to Green Peace and Amnesty International. Papa would suspect they are dope-smoking Communists. Mama thinks PETA is a condiment.

They both suck a meat bone dry. As God is my witness, our parents will never meet.

"I'm late for court." He wrapped his arms around me. "Stay away from Tierney. Give me a day or two to check him out. And keep Cleo with you."

"I have Inga."

Chance pulled me close, tracing his finger over my lips. "Your beagle is likely to eat the evidence. But Cleo's quick with a firearm. And she's not afraid to use it.

Chapter Nine

I jammed across Bridgeport, then slowed to cruise past the Belle Café twice before snagging a parking spot. No California plates on the street. I scooted through the door and checked out the customers.

Belle's catered to the local senior crowd. The day's specials were written on a chalkboard and involved a lot of gravy. I scanned the tables for a mother/daughter team and found just one. They were both collecting Social Security. I ordered a hot chocolate with extra whipped cream to go and a hamburger patty for my partner.

Inga ate her hamburger, and I hunkered down behind the wheel with my cocoa and smartphone. I called every cheap, marginally clean hotel in a five mile radius of the café. Cristina wasn't registered at any of them. But then I wasn't even sure that's the name she would give.

I was running out of ideas. If I struck out at the hotels, I had one last chance to find them at Taqueria La Mexicana. Billy said he was meeting his client there at eleven. I checked my watch. Two hours away. Two whole hours for Cristina to not turn on the radio and zoom full-speed to the Pacific Ocean. I knew the Taqueria makes a mean margarita. I had a sick feeling I'd be drinking my lunch alone.

I poured two fresh waters and tossed the beagle one of Tino's sausages. Then I hauled out Mama's Tupperware and breathed in the gooey pastry. Two cannoli were missing. They were sitting in Billy's stomach in the morgue. I blinked hard and tucked the cannoli away. I fired up the engine.

I was on the lookout for a woman and teenage daughter with California tans. For kicks, I drove by a couple hotels on my list. The buildings were old and worn. They weren't the sort of hotels you'd book on Expedia. And they weren't places Tierney would expect to find his exbartender. They were places you'd bring large quantities of Lysol to. These hotels didn't advertise in the Yellow Pages. They offered weekly and monthly rates. I was guessing some guests never checked out.

I talked to a half dozen desk clerks and struck out. I decided to hit one more sleazy hotel before taking a table at Taquiera's. I flipped a coin and got the Marco Polo Hotel on 26th and Halsted. It wasn't the roughest part of Bridgeport, but I wouldn't stroll down these streets without a big-ass can of pepper spray after dark either.

The Marco Polo was three levels of white brick and stucco. It was built in the sixties and appeared to have resisted updating. I approached the large tinted glass windows and the hair rose on the back of my neck. Something wasn't right. My subconscious connected with something my brain wasn't picking up.

I cut my eyes to the property around the Marco Polo. The street was quiet. Cars crammed for space in the small parking lot. And then I saw it. A big black Lexus sedan, parked on the street in front of the hotel. Inside, two super-sized guys watched the hotel. A cigarette bobbed from the one guy's mouth. The other sucked on a black licorice. I didn't recognize the driver. But I knew beefy boy. He would cheerfully have me for lunch. And I knew the Lexus. It was parked at Tierney's Pub this morning.

I hadn't found Cristina's hotel but Tierney's men had. They had ransacked Bill's office and taken his file. Unwittingly, Bill put Cristina's life in danger. An experienced investigator wouldn't drop a trail of crumbs leading to his client. I blamed his stupid online course for not covering that detail.

I held my breath and drove by the Lexus unnoticed. I turned a hard right at the corner and circled the block. I flipped the cell out of my pocket and punched in my own muscle's number.

"Tino's Deli."

My heart was racing and my voice sounded breathless. "Two of Tierney's men are outside the Marco Polo Hotel. They're waiting for Cristina and her daughter."

Tino's voice tightened. "What are they driving?"

I told him.

"We're fifteen minutes away. Stay in your car. And don't do anything."

I parked on the street behind the Lexus, with three cars and a wide white van between us. The van blocked the driver's side mirror. I scooted undetected around to the trunk where I pulled out my box of tricks. Flinging the box on the passenger seat, I climbed in after it. I pulled out a plum sheath dress, wig, coat, and chocolate kitten heels.

I glanced around. No one in sight. I shoved the seat back, scrunched low, and changed into a blond with my hair cropped short, donning a burgundy double-breasted trench coat. I made the switch before you could say *there's a naked woman in that car*. I polished the look with a pair of dark-rimmed Ferragamo glasses and plum-perfect lipstick. Then I told Inga to guard the car. I threw back my head, tromped past the black Lexus sedan, and proceeded through the doors of the Marco Polo Hotel.

◇◇◇

The young woman at the registration desk buffed her nails, smacked her gum, and pretended not to notice me. Her hair was jet black, face powdered white, and she wore enough black eyeliner to keep Maybelline in business. With her lipstick choice being blood red, I was beginning to wonder if her late night habits involved sucking blood out of unsuspecting strangers when her nasal voice snapped me back.

"*What?*" she demanded when she figured out I wasn't going away.

"I'm supposed to meet Cristina McTigue for lunch, and I don't remember her room number."

"You called me twenty minutes ago." Her eyes dropped to her nails. "Go away."

I wanted to jump over the counter and get the information for myself, but I dropped a fifty on the counter instead. She glanced up and her eyes glazed. She palmed the money.

"The lady still ain't here."

"Maybe I don't know her married name. She has a daughter, about fifteen. I think the girl's name is Halah."

"Room 125." She picked up the phone and punched in the number.

"A woman is in da lobby's askin' 'bout you."

"I'm Bill Bonham's friend. Tell her I'm Bill's—"

Goth girl hung up. "I ain't your social secretary. Tell her yourself."

I trolled over to the window and waited for my A-Team. Six minutes later Tino and Max rolled by like a couple gangstas. Four minutes early. The meatheads didn't glance up. Big bufah.

At the end of the street, Max hopped out and began walking back toward the Lexus. Tino circled the block again. The Buick swung onto Halsted again. It barreled down on the Lexus and braked hard, dead even with the driver's door. Tino spilled out and Max timed a fist in the passenger's face with Tino's elbow in the driver's head. A crescendo of thumps and punches followed. When they were finished, the ex-spies tumbled back into the Buick and drove away. I suspected they'd done this dance before.

I didn't hear the women sneak up behind me. By the time Jimmy Choo perfume clicked in my brain, it was too late. I spun around. The California girls were armed and dangerous. The daughter jetted my face with pepper spray. Her mother nailed me with her lethal brick bag. I went down like a heap of pudding, cradling my head, eyes on fire. I couldn't see, but I heard footsteps running out the door.

And I heard goth-girl smacking her gum.

Chapter Ten

When I opened my eyes, two blurred faces hung over me. I touched the knot on my head and groaned.

"Take her to the hospital. She needs a doctor."

It was Tino's voice.

I sat up and my head exploded. "No doctors. I'm fine." My voice was a squeak.

"Like hell you are."

Tino said, "How much pepper spray hit your eyes? I have a solution in the car to flush them."

Max lifted me in his arms and carried me out the door. A bitter wind off the lake blasted my face. My vision was blurred but I saw, with implicit clarity, two knocked-out-down-for-the-count bullies in a black Lexus sedan.

"They don't look so good," Max said.

"They look great. Is that what they taught you in spy-school?"

Tino smiled. "It was a lucky punch. I'm a humble sausage maker."

"Okay, sure." I said.

Tino barked a laugh. "I'm parked around the corner. You'll drive my car until this blows over. I'm taking yours to the deli."

Geesh. Tino was as bossy as my interfering Italian family.

"My car drives just fine," I said, and thumped Max's chiseled chest. "This is embarrassing. Put me down."

Max said, "We're taking Tino's car. The Buick is bulletproof. You're not."

"Aha! Admit it, Tino. Only thugs and spies drive bulletproof cars. And you're not a thug."

Tino laughed. "The world can be a treacherous place for a sausage maker."

"Max, I am fine. The pepper spray hit my mouth more than anywhere. Put me down, please." He looked into my eyes, seeing my determination. I was going to be put down with or without his help.

"I was enjoying that," Max grinned and lowered my feet to the ground.

Tino handed Max the Buick keys and held out his hand. He wasn't backing down.

"We'll take the Buick," I conceded. "First I have to get Inga. She's in my car."

"I'll take her with me today," Tino said. "We'll make meatballs, and I'll feed her the leftovers."

I squeezed my arms around the ample sausage maker's middle and kissed his cheek. "Thanks, Tino. I didn't know who else to call."

Tino shrugged palms up. "Who else do you need?"

I raised my wrist to my eyes but still couldn't focus through the pepper spray. "What time is it?"

Max peered at my watch. "Ten fifty-four."

I tossed Tino my keys and hooked Max's arm. "Hurry, Max. I hope you like burritos."

◇◇◇

Max weaved in and out of cars. I lost the blond wig, finger-combed my hair, and threw off the coat. By the time Max pulled up to the curb in front of Taqueria La Mexicana, I was slathering my lips with Dr. Pepper Lip Gloss.

"Eleven oh-four," Max said and opened his door. "Let's rock 'n' roll."

I towed him back. "Red Subaru. California plates. There they are."

Max's gaze settled on Cristina. Her sun-kissed skin was like silk. "Hot mama."

"Don't be fooled. Those women are armed and dangerous."

"There's a peace sign on their car, for chrissake."

"That woman's purse packs a punch."

The incident at the hotel had put the women on alert. Cristina had backed her car against the building. She had an uncompromised view of people coming in and an unobstructed escape going out. The engine was idling. Black smoke billowed from the tailpipe. Cristina's fingers drummed the steering wheel. Hot mama wouldn't wait around long. She didn't know it yet, but her lunch date was hanging out with Bogie. Billy Bonham, PI, had eaten his last burrito.

"I'll go talk to her," Max said. "She doesn't like you."

"She's gonna bolt. She'll run you down."

Max flashed a grin and cranked the engine. "You underestimate my charm."

He stomped the gas, veered a hard right, and skidded across the parking lot. The Buick pinned the Subaru to the wall. Max and I spilled onto the pavement running. Flanking the red car, we jerked the rear doors open and fell on the backseat as the wide-eyed women scrambled to lock them.

"Hi, ladies. This wouldn't be necessary if you'd given Cat a chance to talk to you at the hotel."

I poked the daughter's shoulder. "Show your hands, pepper queen."

Mother and daughter twisted their heads around. "You!" The young girl gave me that contemptuous scrutiny only teens can muster. I tried to return the look.

"What's wrong with your face?" Max leaned over, checking for signs of concussion.

I ignored him and turned to hot mama. "I'm Private Investigator Cat DeLuca. Billy asked me to help with your case. This is Max."

"Where's Bill? Why isn't he here?"

My throat caught. Max stepped in.

"I'm sorry to have to tell you that Bill Bonham was murdered last night."

Cristina gasped, stunned. Finally after a long minute, she spoke. "How?"

"He was shot. In his neighborhood, on the street."

Cristina stared out the window. "This is all my fault."

Max shook his head firmly. "The blame rests with the guy who pulled the trigger."

"And the guy who ordered the hit," I muttered.

Halah's breaths came quick and shallow. She gasped for air. Her mom reached across the seat and patted her shoulder.

"Halah Rose hyperventilates."

"Stuff her head in a bag," I suggested.

Max said, "There's more bad news. Someone broke into Bill's office. Your file is missing."

"Holy mother of God." Cristina crossed herself. "What does that mean?"

"The life you created four years ago has been compromised."

"You can't go back to your hotel," I added. "Tierney had two men parked outside. I was trying to warn you when you knocked me senseless."

Cristina winced. "How bad did I hurt you? Do you have a concussion?"

"I've had worse." I tried to give her a smile but my mouth refused to move that direction.

"I'm sorry," she said. "I hope you have insurance."

"Now you're sounding just like my mother," I said.

"My detective is dead. The people I have been running from for four years know where I stayed last night." Cristina did a grimace. "So what's the bottom line? Are you saying we can't go back to California?"

"I'd advise against it," Max said.

Halah wailed. "I *have* to go back. I won't lose all my friends *again*."

Cristina gnawed her lip. "What if it wasn't Kyle. Anyone could've killed Bill."

"*Really?*" I said holding on to my head trying to keep it together. "Bill was walking his mother's dog around her block at midnight. He was probably the only person living within a four-block radius under the age of forty-five. And that's because he was staying with his mom until he got back on his feet. It's not exactly Bridgeport's high crime area."

Max stepped outside and opened Cristina's door. "Whatever you decide, you still have to eat."

Her mouth trembled and the brown, doe eyes welled. Max melted into them. This time my eyes rolled.

"I don't think I can start over," she said.

"Maybe you won't have to," Max said. "We'll figure this out."

Cristina was unsteady, and Max put a strong arm around her and helped her toward the entrance. Maybe it felt good to have a big gorgeous hunky guy shoulder your troubles for a change. Or perhaps the brain tumor made her dizzy. I had to wonder if she should be driving.

Halah Rose glanced around for her bag.

"You won't need your death spray," I said. "I'm buying."

The Taqueria La Mexicana, one of Bridgeport's treasures, is tucked into a building just west of Halsted on 35th. By the time we made our way inside, the lunch crowd was trickling in. The tables were soon filled with people short on time and patience. But at our table, lunch was mostly a quiet, sober affair.

Halah Rose pushed her tostada around her plate.

"You're missing school," Max said.

"The teachers post my homework online. My science teacher videotapes his lectures."

"You're not missing too much, then."

Halah made a face. "Just my winter concert. I made first chair in violin this year."

"Bravo," Max said.

"Then we had to go on this stupid trip." Halah chewed a chip thoughtfully. "I want to play in the Chicago Symphony someday."

"You will," Cristina said.

Max punched a bunch of numbers on his Droid. When he finished, he dropped the cell in his pocket and flashed Halah a pleased grin. "Eight o'clock tonight. Chicago Symphony. Two tickets are waiting for you and your mom in the lobby."

Halah squealed. "OMG! I am *so* psyched!"

"Not tonight." Cristina threw her head back in defiance. "I have plans. I'm finishing what Bill started. I'm going in."

"Whoa," I said. "Bad, bad idea."

"In?" Max said. "In where?"

"It's too risky," I said.

"You can't stop me," Cristina glared.

"Stop what?" Max said.

Cristina dabbed an eye. "Bill was a decent guy. He wasn't afraid of Tierney."

"How did that work for him?" I said.

"I'm not running anymore," Cristina said. "I want my life back."

Halah took a drink of her coke. "Count me in after the concert."

"Seriously?" I said.

Max raked his hair. "What the hell is everybody talking about?"

"Suicide," I said. "Three to five in the pokey."

Halah waved a fry. "My mom says she's breaking into Tierney's Pub tonight."

Cristina sniffed. "That asshole owes me. I'm gettin' back."

Max grinned. "I am *so* psyched."

Chapter Eleven

I texted Cleo. Eight minutes later the canary yellow Corvette whipped into Belle's parking lot and screeched to a stop at our feet.

Halah's eyes widened. "Wow," she said.

Cleo leaned out the window. Her eyes were puffy and red without the help of pepper spray. "Kyle Tierney shot a hole in the greatest guy I ever knew."

"You do realize you met Billy last night." I said.

She pulled out a tissue and blew. "We're gonna bump off that jerkwad. Tonight."

"Bump off?" Halah said.

"Kill," I said.

"We'll do it slow," Cleo said.

"Damn straight," Cristina said.

"Geesh," I said.

Cleo smacked her gum. "Nobody offs Santa and gets away with it. It's like whacking a priest."

I blinked. "A *priest?*"

"Bill wasn't the real Santa, you know," Max said.

"Watch your mouth," Cleo snapped.

She lifted a blanket from the passenger seat and exposed a small arsenal. A Desert Eagle, a Sig Sauer, a Smith & Wesson MP, a Glock, and a Beretta with a pearl handle.

Her eyes gleamed. "I came prepared. What's the plan."

A giant hammer pounded my brain. "*You* are taking Halah to dinner and the Chicago Symphony. Maybe ice cream later. Take her home with you tonight. Bring her by my house in the morning."

Cleo selected the pearl-handled Beretta from the passenger seat and slipped it into her bag. "Good plan. I'll off Tierney in the theatre. Like Abraham Lincoln."

Cristina nodded. "I like it."

I massaged my temples. "Uh, we have a slightly different plan. Halah will fill you in."

Max slipped around to Cleo's passenger door. He gathered the other guns in the blanket and scooped them up in his arms. "I'll keep these in Tino's trunk for you. There's a kid in the car and all."

"I'm not a kid. I'm fifteen!" Halah said, all huffy.

"I was talking about Cleo," Max said.

"Can I drive your Corvette?" Halah asked Cleo.

"Sure."

"She's only fifteen," Cristina gasped.

"You know, she's gotta learn sometime." Cleo slapped an arm around Halah. "But first things first. Girlfriend, we are going shopping."

Halah dove into the passenger seat. "I can't believe I'm going to the symphony."

Cleo kicked the car in gear. "Do you like tattoos?" she said and sped away.

Cristina cringed. "Is my little girl safe with that woman? I mean she's not really unhinged or anything, right?"

I stared at her. Cristina pulled her daughter out of school, drove her across country in an unsound, gutless wonder, checked into a sleazy hotel in a city where a big, bad man was itching to gun her down. I wasn't getting Mrs. Brady here.

"No worries. I'd trust Cleo Jones with my life."

Max and Cristina drove to the deli and swapped the sputtering late-seventies Subaru for Max's Hummer. I tucked my hair under the blonde wig again and drove Tino's bullet-proof Buick back to the hotel. Halah's violin, computer, and clothes were waiting to be rescued on the second floor. Every teenager thinks she can't live without a few things. These were hers. Room 225. The key was in my pocket. I promised I'd get them for her.

The black Lexus sedan that Tierney's guys were driving was parked in front of the hotel. No sign of their sorry, battered faces though. They could be waiting in the lobby, but I doubted it. Whatever plan they had for the missing bartender wouldn't beg for witnesses. I was guessing they got a room. And it would be as close to Cristina's room as possible. Waiting, probably smoking cigarettes and sucking on black licorice whips. Or even worse, waiting in Cristina's room.

I plucked my phone from my pocket and called Mama.

"Caterina, is that you?" Mama doesn't trust caller ID.

"You know it's me, Mama. I wanted to ask if Inga can have a sleepover tonight. You can pick her up at Tino's."

"What's to ask? You should be out with that nice boy from the FBI. The one with insurance."

"I wish, Mama. I'll be working late."

Mama made a disapproving clicking sound with her mouth. "This work of yours. A hootchie stalker. Taking dirty pictures. Seeing things a good Catholic girl should never see." She shuddered.

"Mama, I wish you'd stop telling people I'm a hootchie stalker. I'm a professional private investigator. It's like being a cop."

"A cop without insurance. This life is no good for a girl who should be married and having babies like her sister."

My sister Sophie is a baby factory. She loves to point out that I'm thirty, divorced, and missing all the fun of childbirth. When we were kids, Sophie was busy playing with her perfect little family in her perfect little dollhouse. I was busy skinning my knees and hanging from trees with my brother Rocco. Don't get me wrong. I like kids. And who knows? Maybe someday I'll give Mama grandkids instead of gas. Right now, my future's a mucky blur. I don't know what's gonna happen. But with the way Sophie pumps out those kids, I'm pretty sure her uterus is going to fall out.

Mama groaned. "Oh! There's a horrible, stabbing pain in my chest."

I made a soothing sound. "Oh, Mama. Take some Tums."

"It's not gas. It's a daughter who breaks her mama's heart."

I worked my throbbing temples. "I have to go now, Mama. Thanks for taking Inga."

Mama sniffed. "She wants to come home to grandma. Tino feeds her too many sausages."

I tucked the phone away, slipped out of the car, and made my way to the alley around back. I maneuvered around two big, stinky dumpsters heaped high with garbage. I tried not to breathe. I picked out a wooden crate from one, rotting at the edges, but sound enough to stand on. Scooting close to the brick wall, I counted to the fourth iron-barred window from the left of the building. Cristina and Halah's room. Climbing on the box, tip-toed and craning my neck, I peered through a gap in the curtain. They were still there—the violin was on the dresser, a laptop on the bed. I blew a breath of relief. It appeared Cristina had found refuge in a gentler, more insulated California community. Because somehow, in four years, she'd forgotten the precautions one takes in a big city.

Hugging the wall, I made my way down the row of windows. At each one I dropped the wood box on the cracked asphalt and stretched to spy through the faded curtains. Some rooms were unoccupied. Some guests watched TV. And I saw some things a good Catholic girl shouldn't have to see. At the end of the long row I found what I was looking for. Two beat-up, hamburger-faced guys stretched out on their beds. The driver sucked on a cigarette. Beefy boy's supersized hands gripped a James Patterson thriller. I was mildly surprised he could read.

I trotted back to Tino's car. A woman and her young son tossed a ball on the sidewalk. Her name was Irene. Colby was five, and the tooth fairy has his two front teeth. They were new in town, here from Georgia. Her husband was a mechanic. He was out looking for work.

"Is he any good?"

Irene nodded proudly. "He has a certificate from Universal Technical Institute. But nobody's hiring."

"My mechanic is. He's the best in Bridgeport. Maybe Chicago." I jotted Jack's number on the back of my card. "I'll let Jack know your husband's stopping by."

"How can I thank you?" She looked at the card. "Pants On Fire Detective Agency? Caterina DeLuca?"

"Oops. Wrong side." I flipped the card over for her. "Jack is no picnic to work for. He's tough but he's fair. And he pays his guys well."

"You're a real detective?" She lowered her voice to a whisper. "Is there a mystery at the hotel? Is that why you're here?"

I smiled. "Sort of."

"You're like Kinsey Millhone. I've read all the ABC mysteries." She waved my card. "Maybe I'll call once we're settled. See if you have a little undercover work for me."

"Do that. In fact, I may have a little something right now. It'll take five minutes."

She almost jumped up and down. "What do you want me to do?"

I reached into my bag and pulled out a Benjamin. "For this, I need to borrow your son."

Chapter Twelve

I slid behind the wheel of Tino's Buick and dialed Rocco's number.

"Yo. Cat. Talk to me." My brother believed the caller ID.

"If you and Jackson have a few minutes, I need a favor."

"You got it. Where are ya?"

"At the Marco Polo Hotel. Two of Tierney's thugs are staking the place out. They know Billy's client is here."

"The bartender you told me about?"

"Yeah. Can you do something?"

I heard Rocco smile. "I can make them disappear."

I hung up and unbuttoned my top three buttons. I made up my face to just short of skanky. When I finished, I gazed in the mirror at a $50 ho. Beefy boy wouldn't recognize me. I hardly recognized myself.

The Hummer arrived a few minutes later and snagged a spot in the hotel parking lot. Cristina and Max climbed out, and Cristina hopped in the backseat behind the tinted windows. Max jumped in beside me. He did a double take.

Max whistled. "Damn, girl! I'm all out of twenties."

"Twenty! You call *this* a twenty dollar date?"

Max reached over and touched my blond wig. "I could throw in a burger and a pack of smokes."

Cristina laughed. "You two have great chemistry. How long have you been together?"

I stumbled over my words. "We're not. I mean, not like that. We are just good friends."

"You keep telling yourself that," Max winked.

"Uh hunh," Cristina laughed.

I blushed and tugged at my wig. "Tierney's men took a room down the hall from Cristina's. They don't look so good. You beat them up pretty bad."

"I thought we scared the shit out of them. Why are they still here?"

"Maybe you're not that scary," Cristina said.

"He's plenty scary," I said. "Max was Special Forces. He can kill with his bare hands."

Cristina wet her lips. She wasn't immune to Max's incredible hotness. Max didn't seem to notice. I rolled down my window and sucked a breath of stale, city air before I choked.

"I can't believe those morons are still here," Max said.

I smeared Dr. Pepper Lip Gloss over my red lipstick and smiled. "Not for long, babe."

◇◇◇

The Chicago PD detective car cut to the curb alongside a fire hydrant. The doors opened and Rocco and Jackson trolled across the street. They were, as Chicago cops go, as intimidating as they got. Jackson was Samoan by heritage and built somewhat similar to a brick. And then there was my brother—Italian through and through. He wasn't as massive as his partner, but what he lacked in size he made up for in attitude. They joined Max and me in front of the hotel.

Jackson smoothed my blond wig. "That's a new look for you."

Rocco gave me a quick squeeze. "We're gonna get the guy who killed Bill. Let the ninth precinct handle it. If Tierney's dirty, we'll get him."

"Are you saying Captain Bob considers Kyle Tierney a suspect?"

"Not exactly."

"Cuz this morning Captain Bob blew me off."

Rocco made a face. "Bob blew me off too. I tried to talk to him about the incident at the pub yesterday. He said Billy pissed everybody off."

"I hope he chokes on my donuts."

Rocco said, "Don't go all Rambo on us. We're investigating Tierney on the QT."

"And don't get yourself carried out of his pub again," Jackson said.

Not my proudest moment. "Savino has a big, fat mouth."

Max stared. "You didn't say you were stupid enough to confront Tierney alone."

"Didn't I?"

We stormed the hotel together, Max and I hot on the heels of the Chicago PD. Rocco and Jackson flashed their badges to goth-girl behind the desk. Her gaze lurched to the phone and her fingers twitched. Talk about your big, fat tattletales. I wondered how much the two guys at the end of the hall paid her to squeal if there was trouble. Or if Cristina returned. Clerking at a sleazy hotel can be a surprisingly lucrative job.

I jerked my head toward the phone. "Max, this is Miss Congeniality. She makes too many calls."

"You go ahead. I'll hang here with the hired help."

Goth-girl glared. She reached for the phone and Max clapped a hand over hers. "We like to surprise our friends."

Irene from Georgia closed her book and picked up the toys her son was playing with in the lounge. I pulled a baseball hat and a pair of clear lens glasses out of my pocket and put them on Colby.

"Irene, meet Detectives Jackson and DeLuca from the Chicago PD."

The guys flashed their badges.

"Your son is safe with us," Rocco said. "But it would be best if they don't see you."

I said, "If you'd like to wait in your room, I'll bring Colby right up."

The boy and I followed Jackson and Rocco down the long corridor of wooden doors. We walked past the room with the violin and laptop. I'd return to gather up Cristina and Halah's things. We tromped down the hall to the second door from the end. Colby and I stood well back and off to the side as Jackson pounded on the door.

"Chicago PD. Open up."

"Shit."

The door opened. "We didn't do nothin'."

We came forward then, Colby tightly gripping my hand. Two men glowered. One sucked on a cigarette. There was a small stain around the other man's lip that looked like chew. I suspected it was licorice.

Rocco turned to the boy. "Are these the men who said they'd give you candy if you got into their big black car?"

He laughed, thinking it a game. He nodded.

"That's all we need," Jackson said.

Colby and I retraced our steps down the long, stark hallway.

"This ain't right. The kid's on crack."

"Sir, do you drive a big black car?"

I didn't hear the response. I imagined there was a gulp or two.

"Turn around and place your hands behind your backs. You'll need to come to the precinct for questioning."

"This is bullshit. I know my rights."

"You'll get your phone call." The smile was back in Rocco's voice. "Sir, do you have a permit for these guns?"

"Uh…"

"What's this?" Jackson said.

"Whoa! Those drugs weren't there. You planted them."

"That's what they all say," Rocco said.

Colby swung my hand in his. "I like this game. It's fun to pretend."

"I get to do it all the time."

Chapter Thirteen

Exhaustion blindsided me when I walked through my front door. I'd hardly slept. I had a headache the size Cristina's boulder-bag. The emotional toll of Billy's murder was grueling. I wanted it all to go away. And I wanted to talk to Billy again.

I stripped and stepped into a hot, pulsing shower. I lathered my skin with soft, lavender soap and scrubbed away the slutty layers of makeup. When every last drop of hot water was spent, I slipped into a plush, terry-cloth robe and fell on my bed. Tears welled in my eyes. I was asleep before one hit the pillow.

I didn't know how long I'd slept, but the sky was dark when I opened my eyes. It was the glorious smell of coffee that woke me from a dreamless sleep. And bacon and waffles, I thought. And something else. I sniffed. Fresh strawberries, I decided.

The mattress moved a bit. It wasn't my beagle. I sighed deeply. If a burglar makes me supper before taking off with the silver, I'm putting out the welcome mat.

A hand brushed my hair back and Chance Savino kissed my neck.

"Hmm," I said and rolled over on my back. "I didn't know you could cook."

"I can't. I called my mother."

I sat up with a jerk. "She's here?"

He laughed. "No. She told me to look for a pancake mix in the cupboard."

"And she's definitely not coming?"

"My mom and dad are in India. I think they're visiting a holy man."

I seized his collar with an urgency that surprised me. "I want you to tell them my parents are dead. Say I'm an orphan."

He laughed. "Relax. My parents aren't like that."

"You know, I'll love your parents. But we're talking about my parents here. My family is—I don't know, different. But my parents with your parents? There will be blood."

I knew I was babbling. I couldn't stop.

Savino kissed my mouth. "I like us. I don't really need a visual of our parents meeting right now."

The remnants of my headache were fading fast. He plopped pillows behind my back, and placed the tray in front of me. "Your coffee's getting cold."

A waffle with thinly sliced strawberries and whipped cream seemed to swallow the plate. There was coffee, champagne, and orange juice. A beautiful red rose completed the presentation.

"Champagne? What's the occasion?"

"I was worried about you. It's tough to lose a friend."

"Billy and I were engaged once."

"I'm sorry, honey. I didn't know." Chance wrapped his arm around me.

"We were eight." I looked into his cobalt blue eyes. "I'm going to get Tierney."

"Listen, DeLucky. No going in guns blazing. Let's make sure Tierney's responsible first."

"Oh, he knocked Billy off, alright. I saw it in his eyes."

He kissed my hair. "Give me a day to check him out. I'll let you know what I learn."

There was a definite advantage to having a boyfriend who was with the FBI. I glanced at my plate and smiled. "You get bonus points for the whipping cream."

"And I plan to collect."

Chance mosied to the kitchen, and I heard him stack the dishwasher. I felt a warm tingly feeling rolling southward. I decided it wasn't the waffles. Chance Savino was the full package. Eye candy. And he takes out the garbage. Without being asked.

That's the ultimate turn on. I doubt my ex knew where the garbage can was.

The "candy" word slapped my brain like a big, black licorice whip. It all came slamming back. Beefy boy, the bobbing cigarette dude, Max, the head bashing client, and our devious plans to burgle the pub. *Tonight.*

I shook any remnants of champagne from my head, dashed to my feet, and dropped my robe. I was frantically tugging black jeans over Victoria's leopard-print Secrets when Chance wandered into the room.

"Uh, what are you doing?"

I hopped on one foot, pulling up my jeans. "I'm sorry, babe. I totally forgot I have to work tonight."

"You didn't just say that."

"I really wish I didn't. There's no way I can miss it." I said, stuffing a bite of the waffle in my mouth.

"Yes there is. All you have to do is come back to bed." He walked over, wrapping his arms around my waist, kissing the whipped cream off my lips.

I sighed looking at his perfectly kissable lips. "You are not making this easy."

"I'm not trying to." Chance spoke softly in my ear, while he was making massaging circles with his fingers across my lower back. I knew I was seconds from blowing off my work for the evening.

I pushed off Chance's chest like a springboard and pulled out my evening's attire. I slipped on a black turtleneck and covered it with a black hooded sweatshirt. I took another bite of the waffle and tugged on black socks and soft-soled black shoes.

"Uh, that's a whole lot of black."

"Black is classic."

"My God, DeLucky. Is that a black ski mask in your hand?"

I looked at my hand. "It goes with the flashlight."

"Are you going to tell me what you're up to?"

"Nope."

"Is it because I'd be obligated to arrest you?"

"Pretty much."

"Tell me. Whatever you're doing can't be worse than what I'm imagining."

"It probably is. Don't underestimate me." I winked, taking one last bite of the waffle and a swig of coffee to wash it down.

"I'm sorry about tonight, Chance. I'll make it up to you."

"You have no idea. Be careful out there."

We walked outside and down to the street. "I don't see your car," he said.

"I'm using Tino's car. It's bulletproof."

He groaned. "This just keeps getting better and better."

I put my arms around Savino and kissed him. "Don't worry. And don't wait up for me. I'll be late."

I slipped behind the wheel, started the engine, and rolled down the window.

"Anything else?" he said.

"Leave your phone on. You may have to bail me out of jail."

◇◇◇

It was after eleven when I pulled up to Mickey's. I parked behind a Hummer and checked the hood on my way by. It was still warm. My partners in crime hadn't been waiting long.

Mickey's is my favorite bar. The food is good and if you like cops, the company is too. You don't have to like cops to hang out at Mickey's. But you probably don't want to be a felon.

I know the cops who hang out at Mickey's. A lot are DeLucas. Others are almost like family to me. I know their kids and I go to their birthday parties. Like Captain Bob came to mine. But my friends don't make me crazy. And the alarm on my biological clock doesn't keep them awake at night.

I sailed through Mickey's door and a hand squeezed my bum. I looked back at a half-dozen cops with goofy smiles on their faces. I zoned on the biggest one. Alec Hoard grinned like a boy with mirrors on his shoes. He was having way too much fun.

"You got some quick hands, Alec," I smiled. "Your wife's in my book-club. And do you know what we do in our book club? We talk. We drink good wine. We nosh on good food. But mostly we talk."

"Cat the hootchie stalker," Alec said. "She always knows who's grabbing ass."

The guys at his table roared and slapped Alec's back.

"True." I smiled sweetly. "And for your wife, I will offer my services for free."

And with that, half the bar exploded in laughter.

I caught Max's easy smile across the room. There was something about Max. He had a charisma that drew people to him. He got up from his chair and met me halfway.

He and Cristina had taken a table off to the side where the three of us, surrounded by Chicago's finest, would prepare to execute a felony. I caught my cousin Frankie's crazy laugh before making it to safety.

I waved Max back and faced a herd of four large DeLuca men alone. Papa, Uncle Joey, and Uncle Rudy hugged me. Cousin Frankie weaseled in for a hug, but I effectively cut him off at the pass.

"Ain't you breakin' into the Irish Pub tonight?" Frankie said. "That's what my little birdie tells me."

He was talking about my bird-brain assistant, Cleo.

Papa paled. "Caterina? Is this true?"

"You got a freakin' big mouth, Frankie." I punched his arm. "You don't see my papa standing right next to you?"

"What?" Frankie shrugged and rubbed his arm. "I see him."

Papa is something of a local hero in Bridgeport. His career with the CPD was cut short a few years ago when he was struck down by friendly gunfire in the line of duty. The rookie cop who lost a bullet in Papa's bum is forever banned from Mickey's. And his future on the Force is cemented in traffic duty.

"I know what you're doin'," Frankie said all cocky. "You're going after Tierney for offing Billy. Gonna clean out his safe."

"*What?*"

"Your partner keeps me in the loop."

Papa seized his battle scar. "It's not true, Caterina. Tell Frankie he's crazy."

"That's been documented, Papa." I punched Frankie again.

I summed it up for my cousin. "Frankie, you're a jackass. Cleo is my *assistant*. My *partner* is the beagle. And do you know *why* she's my partner?" I stomped my foot for extra emphasis. "She's the only one who can keep her mouth shut."

That was a lie. I've had complaints from the neighbors.

"I forbid you to go after Tierney," Papa said. "It's insane."

Papa forgets I'm not twelve.

"*Seriously?*" I said.

"She'll be fine," Uncle Joey said. "For the record, Caterina was with us all night. We played poker."

Joey is my favorite uncle. Sometimes he's reckless with the truth. For a cop, he has pockets deep enough to drive a Ferrari. But he has a big heart. And he's on the short list of people I'd call if I was in trouble.

"Poker? Who won?" Frankie asked.

"Me," Uncle Joey grinned. "Let's make it believable."

"I could win," Frankie said.

"Why don't you practice keeping your big mouth shut," Uncle Rudy said.

"Billy was working on an important case," I said. "He'd want me to finish it for him."

"I trust Cat," Uncle Joey said. "She has a good head on her shoulders."

"If your mama finds out…" Papa's shudder pierced through me.

"Deny everything, Papa. You know I will."

Uncle Joey pressed something in my hand. I glanced at the small white card clutched between my fingers.

Robert Beano, Robert Beano and Associates, Criminal Defense Attorney.

"Just in case," my uncle whispered in my ear. "Tell him Joey sent you."

Chapter Fourteen

As I joined my cohorts in crime, a server dropped a big gooey cheese and anchovy pizza on the table. I plopped on a chair, and Max filled my mug with a dark, foamy beer.

"Your papa is staring at Max," Cristina said. "It's creepy."

I smeared my lips with Dr. Pepper Lip Smacker. "Ignore him. His scar itches."

Cristina glanced sideways over her glass. "I think he wants to shoot him."

"Papa's not going to shoot Max. Not unless I'm arrested. Then all bets are off."

Max groaned. "Do all these donut commandos *know* about tonight's operation?"

"Just the DeLucas."

"Great. That explains the hostility."

Cristina shrugged. "Maybe they don't like your C4 explosives."

"Explosives?" I said. "Is that how you crack a safe?"

"Do you have a better idea?" Cristina asked.

I stuffed a bite of pizza in my mouth. "I spent thirty minutes on the Internet. I brought a stethoscope and a center punch."

"I got a hammer and a drill. And energy bars." Cristina nudged her head in Papa's direction. "We might have to accept the fact that the mission is compromised."

I didn't forget for a moment that I'd dissed a really great guy to be here. I could be home smothered in whipping cream, and heady with champagne. But I was on a mission. Tonight was for Billy. I was Phyllis Marlowe. No way was I going home empty handed.

Max drained his beer. "What's your point, Cristina?"

"If the cops are on to us, maybe we should pull out. Abort the operation."

"You know this isn't really a covert op," I said.

"I know you don't bring C4 to a bake sale."

Max said, "What do you say, Kitten? Do we abort?"

I shook my head. "Let's light this puppy up."

We parked in the alley behind the Pub. Max unscrewed the dome light, and we scrunched down low in our seats.

Cristina leaned forward from the backseat. "When Billy called me last night, he told me he bombed at the pub."

"Uh yeah, you could say that." I made a face. "Santa stripped to his skivvies while running for the streets of Chicago. Captain Bob's grandkids need therapy."

"I decided we need a better plan," Cristina said.

"Put a lot of thought into that one, did ya?"

She let that slide. "After I got the call from Bill, I came here and hid in the alley. I needed to find another way in."

I couldn't begin to count how many kinds of stupid her Santa charade was. I could only hope this one was better.

"What would that be? A secret entrance? Let me guess. A brick you push and a door magically opens," I snapped.

"You're not helping," Max muttered next to me.

"Sorry." I muttered back loud enough for Cristina to hear it.

The truth is, I blamed Cristina for Billy's death. But I blamed myself more. Kyle Tierney was a dangerous man. And Bridgeport is a tight community. It's not exactly rocket science to identify a face from the past behind Santa's beard. I should have anticipated Billy was in grave danger. Instead I drank tequila and danced to "Hotel California." I could have saved my friend.

Cristina ignored my petty comments. "At 1:45 a.m. the cook takes the trash to the dumpster. Some things don't change. It was just as I remembered."

"And this helps us how?"

"It's all part of my plan. When the cook comes out, I'll sneak past him and slip inside. There's a utility sink by the back door. I'll duck under the sink."

"You will what?"

"I'm double jointed—a freak of nature. I fold up in a small ball."

"Wow," Max said. "Now that's a party trick."

Cristina laughed. "I never lost a game of hide and seek."

Cristina hiked her bag with the hammer, drill, and energy bars onto her shoulder. She stepped out of the car and scampered to the left of the Pub's door. At 1:38 the back door opened. A man with two big garbage bags appeared in the doorway. Cristina pulled the ski mask over her face. When he stepped to the dumpster she slipped behind him, and through the door.

I blew a sigh. "There goes the human pretzel."

"Yowsa," Max smiled.

He drove around front and parked across the street several doors down from Tierney's. I poured two coffees and opened Mama's Tupperware of cannoli while the bartender inside counted the till.

The Hummer's back doors opened. In a flash, Max and I twisted around and faced the backseat. Locked and loaded.

Max waved a Desert Eagle. I brandished my Dr. Pepper Lip Smacker.

"You're scaring me, girlfriend," Cleo said.

"Dammit." I removed the cap and smeared my lips.

Max swallowed a smile. "Take the twin out of my glove box. Now you got one for the night. Just hope to God you don't have to use it. It has one hell of a kick back, babe."

"That's a big-ass gun," Cleo said. "I want one."

I said, "Aren't you supposed to be getting ice cream somewhere far far away?"

"No way," Halah said. "We're your getaway drivers."

"You don't drive," I reminded her.

"She does now. She's a quick learner." Cleo said.

Halah giggled. "Told you the Xbox racing games helped."

"She gave me some tips on how to tag cars to make them flip around. I am gonna pick myself up an Xbox 360 tomorrow."

"Fabulous, Cleo. Just what you need."

"Be nice," Max said. "They're fifteen."

We watched the staff wipe down the last tables and clean up the bar. When they had finished, they bundled their coats, locked the door, and disappeared in their cars.

"Showtime," I said.

Max drove around back. He tossed Cleo his keys saying, "Park around front. You got me? Call if we get company."

Cleo snorted. "Don't worry. If it's Tierney, I'll just blow his head off."

"Hey, I want a gun," Halah whined in a way only a teen can.

Cleo reached into her bag.

"Don't you dare," I said between gritted teeth and tossed back my Lip Smacker. "Here, you can take mine."

Max and I pulled masks over our faces and grabbed our tools. We ran for the back door.

Cristina pushed it open and pulled us inside.

She led us through the kitchen to a dimly lit hallway with four or five doors on either side. A door at the end of the corridor would open to the pub. There would be a sign on the other side—Staff and Leprechauns. At the second door on our left, Cristina stopped and stretched on her tiptoes. Tracing her finger along the door frame, she dragged down a key.

She opened the door. "Kyle is a man of habit. He hates change. Four years later, he's got the same code on his security alarm."

She hit the light and we stepped inside. It was a man's room. No fluff. Lots of rich browns, deep green, and leather. A wet bar, a single round oak table, and comfy chairs for long nights of high stake poker. It's where Billy was busted fondling the safe. And where Kyle Tierney killed a man.

Max hung a stethoscope around his neck. I unzipped my bag.

"Only a handful of people know about the safe," she said.

Cristina crossed the room to a painting of a Dublin pub. She removed the picture, revealing a small high security wall safe with a dial combination lock.

"Blow it up," she said to Max and scooted back.

I dragged out my drill. "I got this. YouTube 101."

Max explored the safe with gloved hands while I flexed my drill. He put the stethoscope to the dial, gently spun the lock, and the door swung opened.

Cristina giggled. "Hot damn. Smokin' Double OOOH Seven."

"It wasn't locked." I added *brain surgeon* under my breath.

The stacks of money Cristina remembered were gone. No jewelry. No books—cooked or otherwise. Just a single sheet of paper. Max removed it from the safe and read out loud.

"Cristina. I knew you'd come. You have something that belongs to me. And now I'm coming for you."

Max cocked a brow.

"What the hell?" I said.

She shuffled a foot. Like a kid caught with her hand in the cookie jar.

Her eyes went blink blink. "I suppose it could be the earrings."

My teeth clenched. "The earrings you said belonged to you."

"It's a long story."

"And I will choke it out of you." I stuffed my drill in the bag and zipped. "*After* we blow this gin joint. If Tierney's expecting you, he could know we're here."

A muted sound seeped from the kitchen. It was the back door. My heart skipped to my throat.

Max whispered, "You're a freaking 1-900 psychic."

The bad guys were coming. There was nowhere to run. And I'd given my Lip Smacker to Halah.

Max pointed to the bar. In a flash, Cristina was behind it.

I hesitated.

Max pulled the Desert Eagle from inside his jacket. He mouthed; *"I'll take the first four."*

"Show-off," I mouthed back while heaving my own Desert Eagle from the back of my black jeans.

He killed the light and pressed against the wall by the door. I ducked under the table and waited.

There was whispering. And then quiet footsteps in the hallway, moving closer and closer. A strange tension built in my chest and I willed myself to breathe. I trained my eyes on the doorway and aimed low.

There were two of them. Meaty guys with guns and shadowed faces. They stopped at the door and listened. One shifted his piece to the other hand and took a step inside. He twisted his thick neck around the door frame. Max hit him dead center on the back of his neck. He dropped in a big ol' heap of stars.

Before the second guy could react, Max shuffled a step and plowed his face with a full-on punch. He went over backwards. The floor delivered the final blow.

Cristina peered from behind the bar all googly-eyed. Blink blink.

"Hot damn, Double Oh Seven."

I high-fived the air. "It was a team effort."

Max grabbed my arm and Cristina scampered behind us. We stomped over the sleeping trolls, hotfooted down the hall and through the door that opened to the pub. We escaped in the wake of leprechauns and St. Nick. Breaking out the front door, we jerked off our masks on the other side.

The Hummer was parked in front of the pub. We tumbled inside and the look-out duo squealed.

Halah said, "That's what I'm talkin' about! No one gets in on our watch." She karate-chopped the air. "We wudda whacked 'em good."

Cristina's hands trembled. She cracked open a bottle of Jameson she had snagged from behind the bar.

"Kyle's finest," she said.

Cleo hauled out a Beretta pistol and blew on the barrel. "Nobody gets past the Pants On Fire Posse."

Cristina tipped the bottle to her lips and gulped. "Shut up," she said.

There was the sound of an engine cranking and headlights flashed across the street. A red Ferrari merged with the traffic. I did a double-take. And laughed. Uncle Joey shot a thumbs-up cruising by.

Chapter Fifteen

I woke the next morning with a song spinning in my head.

Georgia On My Mind…

My pillow hinted of peach shampoo and aftershave. I reached for Savino and got nothing. One eye squeezed open. 9:09. Special Agent Chance Savino was long gone. He'd be on his third coffee and second yogurt by now.

I cuddled up in the blankets and hummed a little. I thought about coffee and donuts. And Georgia.

"Arrrrgh!"

Georgia! I lunged for the phone and punched some numbers.

"Jack's Auto Repair."

"Hey. Jack. This is Cat DeLuca."

He grunted. "Matt from Georgia was here when I arrived at seven."

Ouch. "I promised his wife I'd call.'"

"That's what he said."

"Tell him I'm sorry. I worked late and—"

"I told him you were unreliable. And dangerous."

Geesh! Dorothy again.

"Jack, I'm sorry the bad guys blew up Dorothy. But it wasn't me."

"She was a good car. The best car."

"Dorothy's with your dad now," I said, and paused a moment out of respect. "What about Matt from Georgia? Did you give him a job?"

"He's working on a transmission now. The kid knows what he's doing."

I felt a surge of relief. "Right on. They'll be able to move out of that awful hotel."

"Matt didn't say anything about a hotel. I'll ask around. I might be able to find something for him."

I expected no less. "Thanks, Jack."

"Words are cheap, Caterina. I want your mama's cannoli."

"Done."

"My nephew Devin was released from treatment yesterday. I'm proud of him. He'll have a fresh start."

"Uh huh."

"The guys at the shop are having a party for him. I want you to come."

"God, no."

"I don't like your attitude."

"Your nephew is dangerous."

"No one's perfect."

"He tried to kill me."

"So you're the one holding a grudge now."

I opened my mouth to say something and a sound came out. Like the gnashing of teeth.

"Devin has changed," Jack said. "You'll see at the party."

"I won't be there."

"You'll come or you're cut off."

"You wouldn't!"

"I'll never look under your hood again."

I exaggerated a sigh. "If I come, do I get a free oil change?"

"No. And there's something else you should know. I'm not making excuses for Devin here. But sometimes people want to kill you."

"That hurts, Jack."

"I don't know how to say this."

"Please don't."

"But I feel I need to say it for your own good."

"Here we go."

"Caterina," Jack sighed. "You bring it out in people."

◇◇◇

Mama was feeding Inga breakfast when I rolled into her kitchen. I looked in her bowl and salivated. Sick.

"My grand-dog eats what Oprah's dogs eat," Mama said proudly. "Oprah feeds her dogs chicken, brown rice, and carrots."

I looked again. "Isn't that chicken cacciatore?"

"With organic carrots. Like Oprah."

"I don't see brown rice. Is that pasta?"

"Oprah's dogs are not Italian."

I don't know about my siblings. But in my next life, I'm coming back as my parents' dog.

"Thanks for taking care of Inga."

"My granddog wants another sleep-over."

I looked at Inga. She slid closer to Mama. Or the chicken cacciatore. I couldn't tell which.

"If she stays here much longer, she won't be able to fit through her doggy door."

Mama shook her head and made that tsking sound with her mouth. "*Chepreca*. Rocco's girls wanted to take her to the dog park."

Inga fetched her leash and danced with it.

It was two against one. I caved. "Okay mama, have fun. But bring a poop bag to the park. Nobody can eat that much chicken cacciatore."

Mama stuffed a casserole dish in my arms. "Take this to Billy's mama. You should talk. You were the last person to see him alive."

"Uh, no I wasn't. That would have been the killer."

"Mrs. Bonham said you brought Billy home drunk."

"I can only hope he died happy."

Mama crossed herself. "Death follows you, Caterina. Father Timothy thinks you owe Mrs. Bonham an apology."

I cringed. "When did you tell Father Timothy?"

Mama reached for the phone and pushed the speed dial. "I'm telling him now."

I fled with Mrs. Bonham's casserole.

◇◇◇

I steeled myself as I drove to the house where Billy grew up. Mrs. Bonham was a formidable woman. As far as I knew, she never smiled. Her chocolate chip cookies will crack your teeth.

Mrs. Bonham wasn't friendly when I was Billy's best friend. Now she thought I was responsible for Billy's death. I already blamed myself. I didn't need a pointing finger.

I tiptoed up the Bonham steps and softly rapped my knuckles on the door. I was fully prepared to drop the casserole and run. But the dog gave me away. That dog has a big mouth. Unless you're talking about who killed Billy. He was the only one who knew. And he wasn't talking.

Her eyes were red and swollen when she opened the door. Grief seemed to have diminished her. Mrs. Bonham appeared less daunting now.

"I'm sorry for your loss. Billy was a terrific guy."

That unleashed a new torrent of tears.

I thrust the casserole dish toward her and she took it. "I brought chicken cacciatore. With organic carrots."

She lifted the lid and peeked inside. "It's beef stroganoff. My favorite."

And I thought Mama only knew everything about me.

"Come in, Caterina. I want to ask you something."

This couldn't be good. I groaned inwardly and dragged my feet inside.

Mrs. Bonham gestured toward a chair and I sat. There were two used cups and a plate of chocolate chip cookies on the coffee table.

"Father Timothy just left. He loves my cookies."

Of course he does. He's got dental insurance.

She whisked away the dirty cups and returned with fresh coffee.

I said, "I didn't know Billy was back in town until I ran into him the other day."

Her face softened. "He told me. At least you had a little more time with him."

"If I'd realized he was in danger—"

"There's nothing you could have done. Captain Bob thinks it was a drive-by shooting. I get the feeling he's not losing any sleep over it."

"Captain Bob is an idiot."

Mrs. Bonham blew her nose. "Billy loved you. I always hoped you'd be my daughter-in-law one day."

I was speechless. Mrs. Bonham had been stiff around me. I thought she didn't like me.

She passed the plate of cookies. "Have another one, dear."

I took a cookie and broke off a bite with my incredibly strong fingers. "Mmmmm."

Mrs. Bonham smiled at my nummy noises. "Billy never had a lick of sense. He married a little tramp from Kansas. Nicole something. She showed up here last night. Can you believe the nerve of that hussy?"

I nodded. "Billy said his wife was from Oz."

"He called her the Tin Woman. No heart. She wasted no time getting here."

"What did she want?"

"She said Billy had the birthday present he gave her last year. She wanted to look in his room."

"Did she?"

"Over my dead body. The little tramp broke his heart."

"Did Nicole say what she was looking for."

"Diamond earrings. Isn't that a hoot?"

"You didn't believe her."

"She's a cheap, shiny-bauble-kind-of-girl. She wouldn't know real diamonds if she held them in her hand."

Billy was a sucker when it came to women. He deserved better than that.

"I know for a fact that Billy bought a bowling ball for her last birthday. My son was between jobs. I let him use my credit card."

Billy told me his wife was after the earrings ever since he foolishly told her about them. Even so, I found her rush to Chicago odd.

"If you see Nicole again, would you call me?"

I wanted to know where the Tin Woman was when Billy was killed.

"Of course." She gave a sad smile. "Billy said you're a great detective."

I stood to go. "Mrs. Bonham, you said there was something you wanted to ask me."

"I want you to find the bastard who killed my son."

I slid behind the wheel of Tino's Buick with a plastic baggy of tooth-cracking chocolate chip cookies. My cell phone blared "Your Cheatin' Heart." I glanced at the number and didn't recognize it.

"Pants On Fire Detective Agency. We catch liars and cheats."

"What about big freakin' loud mouths? A woman like that hanging around my building ain't good for business. Ya know what I mean?"

"Who is this? What are you talking about?"

"This is Hal Irving, the landlord at Bohnam's office." I heard bushy brows darting up and down. "I need you to get down here. Now. There's a psycho chick storming up and down the halls, throwing a bloody damn temper tantrum that Bill's not in. I don't want the bacon brigade rolling through here."

When police get called to this part of town, they come with more than just one or two cop cars. And someone always gets a free ride to the slammer.

"Okay, I'm on my way. What's she doing there?"

"Says she's got an appointment with Bill. She's freaking the hell out. I tell her 'he hasn't been around and he's not answering his phone.' Is he freakin' sick or something?"

"He's something."

"So what the hell am I supposed to do with this freakin' butterfly lady."

"Butterfly lady?"

"Tell Billy to get his shit together. This ain't my problem. And if the Five-O get called, he's out on his ass."

"I'm almost there."

I zoomed across Bridgeport and parked in front of Billy's office in a police only zone. I reached in the glove box and slapped my official police sticker in the window. It was Rocco's. He finally quit looking for it after a while.

A woman in designer jeans and trailing furs paced the side-walk in front of Billy's office. Her hair was candy-apple red, a color you don't see in nature, and a butterfly tattoo was poised to fly off an ivory breast. Her French perfume was too rich for me to name, and she smelled like cheeky-barmaid-marries-rich-old-fart money.

She stomped a pouty foot. "Billy's late. I'm Sylvia. I don't like to be kept waiting."

"No one does." I unlocked the door and she followed me inside

"Be a darling and put this somewhere."

She flung the fox from her neck and I sidestepped. The little guy landed limply on Billy's desk. The marble eyes stared at me pitifully. I shuddered.

The woman was faux from her toe cleavage to her fake eye-lashes. And I had questions about the girls launching the butterfly.

"Faux is a good look for you," I said looking at her ridicu-lously long nails. "You should try it in fur. You've got it down in everything else."

Sylvia raked me with her eyes. She took in my hoodie, yoga pants, running shoes, and chestnut hair clutched in a ponytail.

My day hadn't started well. After my cheery conversation with Jack, I dressed for my morning run. My running partner ditched me for a bowl of chicken cacciatore. I missed my run and my shower. Somewhere along the way, I had added Dr. Pepper Lip Smacker and a few swipes of mascara. I hoped I had wiped the sleep from my eyes.

"So you're Bill's hotshot partner."

She said it like I wasn't hot at all.

"Private Investigator Cat DeLuca. I'm a lot hotter after a shower."

She was unconvinced.

I made coffee and filled two large red mugs. "Cream? Sugar?"

"Whiskey, if you have it. It's gotta be five o'clock somewhere in the world."

I found a bottle in Billy's drawer and glanced at my watch. In Chicago it wasn't even noon.

"It's five in France," I said.

Sylvia splashed bourbon in her coffee and clinked her cup against mine.

"*Santé!*"

She dropped in a chair, and I sat beside her. She fidgeted with her ring and I shielded my eyes. Her rock could blind like a playboy calendar in a frat house.

"How can I help you?" I said.

"I'm afraid you'll take me for a fool."

Too late, I thought, siding with the fox. "Try me."

"I need your services tonight."

"Tonight isn't good for me. I have plans."

My plans included a bubble bath, a bottle of wine, and maybe a sexy comedy on Netflix. And then I was taking two hunky guys to bed with me. Ben & Jerry. Frankly, I was looking forward to both guys.

It had been a crazy couple of days. I was still reeling from Billy's murder. I closed three cases this week. And if I had to see one more fumbling lover through the lens of my camera I'd—

"It has to be tonight. I'm getting married Friday."

"*This* Friday?"

She stuffed something in her mouth and chewed fiercely. "Nicotine gum. Supposed to help you quit."

"Does it help?"

"Does it look like it helps?" she snapped. "I'd kill for a cigarette. Before this crap with Garret, I hadn't smoked in years."

"Who's Garret?"

"He's the piece of shit fiancé I'm supposed to marry Friday." Sylvia sucked her gum fiercely. "A drunk truck driver smeared my Howie's body all over the Ike. I sued his ass off. And now guess who shows up wanting a share of my grieving money."

"Uhm…"

"Howie's gold-digging family! Hell, I didn't meet half of 'em 'til he was dead." She stuffed more gum in her mouth. "I didn't ask for the motherload. It's not like I pushed Howie into traffic."

"It's not like he was a fox."

"I hate Howie's family. I want you to off 'em all."

I gasped. "Kill them?"

"I want you to *talk* to Howie's family and make them go away."

"I thought you meant—"

"That was harsh, Cat. I don't like your methods."

Sylvia was possibly the most unlikeable female I'd met since my sister Sophie was born and moved into my bedroom.

"Where's Billy? He promised to help me."

"Billy's away."

"We had a deal. I already paid him."

"I'll refund your money."

"Not interested."

"I'll double it."

She shook her head stubbornly.

"I have to be honest with you," I lied. "Billy has gone on a vacation. I mean a really long vacation. And I can't help you. I catch cheaters. I don't negotiate with other people's families. I have enough problems with my own."

"Who said anything about negotiating with Howie's gold-digging family? I told you I was here about my *fiancé*. You should take notes."

She shoved a picture in my face.

"Holy hot guy," I breathed.

The photograph was taken somewhere tropical with white sand, palm trees, and a shared beach blanket. It was easy to understand why Sylvia fell for the piece of shit fiancé. Garret was a hunk with four-pack abs and a disarming smile. His arm was slipped loosely around Sylvia's shoulder and the butterfly,

I noted, wasn't her only tattoo. Sylvia tucked the photo back in her purse.

Her lip trembled. "After my husband Howie was creamed by that truck—"

"And you became filthy rich," I soothed her.

She nodded. "I met Garret. He had moved in, and I planned the wedding. But then last week I found Garret going through my financial statements. I was furious but he blew me off. Said he was looking for stationery. Ha!"

"You didn't believe him."

"There's a fat stack on the desk." She slugged down the last of her drink. "Last night Garret stayed out late. When he came home, he reeked of cheap perfume."

My head hurt. "What do you want from me?"

"I want you to tell me if I should marry Garret."

"Whoa."

"I have to know I'm not making a terrible mistake."

Sylvia didn't need me to tell her the truth about her fiancé. In my experience, women know when a partner is chipping. We don't always trust our gut. I know this because my gut was screaming at me when my ex was boinking one of the waitresses at his restaurant. One day they passed me on South Throop Street. I actually fell for Johnnie's "she was picking up an empty soda bottle" line.

Sylvia reached for me, and I sat on my hands. "Garret is meeting a friend at Bernice's Tavern at eight. Get close enough to hear what they're talking about. Let me know how he acts around women when I'm not around."

It sounded easy enough. At least no naked pictures were involved.

I said, "I should warn you I've had more experience with men you wouldn't want to marry."

She laughed and splashed Billy's bourbon in my coffee.

And just like that, I watched my bath bubbles disappear.

Chapter Sixteen

I jetted home for a quick shower and a change of clothes. I blow-dried my hair and slipped on a three-quarter sleeve blouse and a pair of skinny jeans. I sat in my office and was checking emails when the phone rang.

It was Savino. "Hey, Babe. I met Kyle Tierney. He has a rock-solid alibi for the night Billy was killed."

"Of course he has. He's a liar."

"He also has security footage at his house. He was in at eight. Didn't step outside until five the next morning."

"Tierney ordered the hit. He's guilty as the schmuck who pulled the trigger."

"Maybe."

"Cristina told Billy what really happened. Tierney had to waste him."

"Why? He served his time. Billy's testimony didn't have any punch. Hearsay. It wouldn't stand up in court."

"I can't believe you're defending him."

"Kyle Tierney is a calculating guy. He's not impulsive. He's not going to order a hit on a guy in a Santa suit for pissing him off. If he had Bonham killed, there's a solid motive we haven't uncovered yet."

"You can bet your cute ass there is."

I heard Savino smile. "How much do you really know about Billy's client?"

"Uhm…"

"There could be more to the story than she's telling. Did you check her out?"

A professional guffaw on my part. "Nope."

"You've been through a lot, Cat. And you were taking over for Billy. I'm sure Cristina was convincing. You want me to run a background check?"

"No, that's okay. I'll have Rocco take care of it."

I glanced around the seat and smiled. Cristina had left a soda can in the car.

"I have her prints."

My brother picked up on the first ring. "Yo."

"I need to see you, bro. Where can we meet?"

Jackson mumbled something in the background.

"My partner's hungry," Rocco said. "We can meet at Mickey's."

"Gotcha. On my way."

"Last one there buys lunch."

"You're almost there, aren't you?"

"Walking in the door. Jackson says, bring mucho dinero. He could eat a horse."

"Order for me. Extra peppers. Hold the horse."

Ten minutes later I skated into Mickey's with Cristina's soda can in a zip-lock baggie. Our server was just serving heaping plates of golden fried chicken, mashed potatoes and gravy, and coleslaw.

Jackson leaned over, took half the chicken off my plate, then pocketed the soda can. "Evidence from another slap and tickle?"

For some strange reason, the Chicago PD doesn't take my Pants On Fire Detective Agency seriously.

"Don't listen to him, sis. He knows you're good at what you do."

"It's true," Jackson winked. "I like dirty pictures."

I made a face.

Jackson said, "Rocco's playing nice cuz his birthday's coming up. He wants you to babysit a few days."

"Cool. My house rules stand. The girls get ice cream every night."

"Just don't tell Maria. And I need tickets for the Bears/Forty-niners game. We're flying to San Francisco for my birthday."

"I'm guessing the game's sold out."

"Is that a problem?"

"Nope. I just want you to be grateful." I emptied my wine glass. "I saw Mrs. Bonham this morning. She wants to know what's going on with the investigation. What do you have?"

Rocco blew a sigh. "I can tell you what we don't have. Not a witness, a weapon, or a motive. It's like somebody shot Billy and disappeared into thin air."

"But you have the man responsible. Billy's death is on Kyle Tierney. I'm sure of it."

Rocco opened his mouth to say something and changed his mind. He stuffed in a mouthful of mashed potatoes instead.

"Captain Bob was right about one thing," Jackson said. "Bonham bought trouble like a horse draws flies."

Rocco smiled. "Billy loved the ladies. They bought him more than a little trouble. If you're right about Tierney, this bartender chick could have been the final ticket that checked him in to the wooden Waldorf."

"Billy was a sucker for a good-looking woman," I admitted. "Here's an example. Last week two blonds picked him up at a bar. They took him home to play strip poker."

Jackson said. "How can I meet these women?"

"Bonham?" Rocco said doubtfully. "There had to be a whole lotta alcohol involved."

"Women loved Billy. He was down to one sock and his undies when one of the women screams that her husband is home. They push him out a window in his tightie whities. He couldn't get his stuff back."

"Ouch. The dumbass got hustled."

"That's what I told him. But he still didn't get it. Billy thought those blonds were crazy about him. It's just as well, I suppose.

He was going through a messy break-up. His ego needed a few strokes."

"That's a full-fledged beating," Rocco said. "I'll ask around at the station. There could be other incidents."

"Keep it on the down-low," Jackson said. "We don't want to piss off Captain Bob any more than he already is."

"What's wrong with Bobby?"

"He's getting a lot of pressure from the guys upstairs about the Bridgeport Bandit. Jackson and I have been after this guy for weeks. Nada. We're getting reamed by the press."

I said, "If you want some help, I—"

"We got it handled," Jackson said hastily.

I pointed to the bulge in his pocket. "Those are Cristina's fingerprints. I appreciate you running them for me."

Rocco and Jackson looked at each other, then me. "Why?"

"I'm not sure her story is adding up. Cristina said Tierney had her diamond earrings. So we, uh, kind of broke into his safe."

"*You broke into the Irish Pub?* Dammit, Cat. Bob told you to stay away from Tierney."

"He wasn't there."

If my brother's fingers weren't busy with a chicken breast, he might have tried to shake some sense into me.

"In case you were interested, the results were zip on the earrings. But Tierney left a note in the safe for Cristina. It said she has something that belongs to him."

"What?"

"The diamond earrings."

"You said Tierney had them."

"That's what Cristina thought. And Tierney thinks Cristina has them."

"So where the hell are they?"

I shrugged. "The note said he was coming for her."

"That's a threat." Rocco said.

Jackson deadpanned, "Do you want to report the threat you found in Tierney's safe to Captain Bob?"

"You're hilarious."

"It looks like Cristina was shaking more for Kyle Tierney than his martinis," Rocco said. "Makes you wonder what else she's lying about."

Jackson grunted. "If Tierney left a note, he expected her to break in. But why? Not for the earrings."

"A couple of his guys were waiting too,"

"Dammit, Cat." Rocco said.

"No worries. We roughed them up a little, knocked them senseless."

Rocco said, "You and Cristina managed this?"

"Cleo was at the symphony."

"Uh huh."

"And she was out of buckshot anyway."

Jackson was all bug-eyed. "Damn, girl."

I thought steam would come out of Rocco's ears. He blew air instead.

"Thank Max for me. I owe him for this one."

Chapter Seventeen

My fox-killing client suspected her fiancé was cheating on her. But there wasn't time for 8x10 glossies. The caterers were already frosting the cake. I wouldn't be able to tell Sylvia what Garret was up to last week. But I could give him the chance to man-up tonight. He could prove to Sylvia that he loves her. Or not.

I cracked out the serious ammo—sassy, sexy, and just a half-inch short of slutty.

I tromped into the Bernice's Tavern a little after four in red-hot stilettos and a little black dress. The dress was a Roxanne Barbara original and a study in leg and cleavage. Guaranteed to smoke out guys who aren't blind, committed, or gay.

Or, you know, getting married Friday.

I recognized Sylvia's piece of shit fiancé from the hunky beach blanket photo she showed me in Billy's office. His steel-gray eyes caught mine in the bar mirror. I looked away. He nearly whiplashed his fine self rubbernecking around.

I sat at a small table in line with the mirror over the bar and slid a gold cigarette lighter beside me. The "lighter" was a voice activated recorder—a gift from the much hunkier Savino.

I glanced at the drink menu. When I looked up, the piece of shit fiancé hovered over me. Two drinks in his hand.

"Hi, gorgeous. If you're waiting for someone, here I am."

Seriously? Did Sylvia actually fall for such a cheesy line?

"I have a date," I said. "He's late."

"Is that a problem?"

"It is if he wants to get laid."

"I like that. You've got fire."

Was this guy for real? I had to wonder how someone—even my loony tunes, fox-killing client—got mixed up with this hustler.

"Let's make him jealous." He dropped his bum in a chair and slid us both a martini. "Why waste a perfectly good happy hour just because your date is a—"

"Putz?"

He wrapped his arm around the back of my chair. "I'm Garret."

"Cat." I traced a finger on the rim of my glass. "The last stranger who bought me a drink turned out to be married."

"Not guilty." He held up his left hand.

"Girlfriend?"

"Can I answer that in the morning?" His fingertips danced along my arm.

Gag me. The thought of spending the night with him made me want to hurl.

Garret leaned close and his lips twitched a smile. "The night is young. Who knows how it will end?"

Actually, I did. And so did he. He was going home to Sylvia. She owned the big house, and she paid the bills. Her grieving money probably bought the martinis on the table. The only thing I didn't know was if I'd get out of there before smacking the creepy grin off his face.

I downed my drink and flexed my fingers. A few more of those and I'd go for his throat.

With an intimate gesture, Garret pulled two cigarettes from a pack and held one to my lips. I shook my head.

"I don't smoke."

His curious gaze dropped to the gold lighter on the table.

"I'm quitting. The lighter's like a familiar friend." I scooped it up quickly and stood.

"You're not leaving?"

"I am."

Garret's hand restrained me. "Wait. How can I reach you?"

"We could meet here Friday," I said all straight-faced.

Like between the wedding and the reception.

He exaggerated a sigh. "Unfortunately, I'm leaving on a business trip this weekend. I'd like to call you when I get back. You and me, we got something special here."

"Do we?"

"We do." He drained his glass. "I got a feeling the gods are smiling on me tonight."

"Yeah?"

I dropped the lighter in my bag and slung it on my shoulder. Leaning low, I whispered in his ear.

"Cuz I got a feeling the gods are laughing their socks off."

I slid behind the wheel and the smell of sausages filled my nostrils. I wasn't alone. Fear froze everything but my eyeballs. A distinct wheezing sound came from the backseat. Inga was at grandma's. And she didn't have sinus troubles. But I knew who did.

My gaze whipped to my rearview mirror and I jumped.

Devin waved a sausage at me.

I opened my mouth twice before a sound came out. Then I reached over the backseat and slugged him with my bag.

"Get out. You scared the crap out of me."

Devin snorted a laugh. I put the bag away. He clambered over the seat and plopped down beside me.

"I was just released from treatment. They let me out early for good behavior."

I could smell the stench of cheap alcohol on his breath. I put the key in the ignition and rolled down the windows. The treatment did wonders.

"Yeah, right. They don't let you out of rehab for good behavior, dumb ass. You escaped."

Devin twisted his mouth. "You DeLucas think you're so effin' perfect."

"*Seriously?* Have you met my effin' perfect family?" I closed my eyes and counted to ten. When I opened them again he was still there. "Why are you here, Devin?"

"I want to make things right between us."

"Good luck with that."

He threw me a look. "You're not helping me with this situation here. I think it's the least you could do."

I bit my tongue. "Really? Please, continue."

"I can't remember much about that night—"

"That's convenient."

"I'm guessing things ended pretty badly."

He waited for me to say something. I pressed my lips together to keep from screeching like a crazy person.

He finally said, "This is awkward."

I screeched like Cleo. "Awkward? You tried to *kill* me. You crashed my thirtieth birthday party. *I didn't get cake!*"

"Chill, Cat. I'll buy you a cake. I've changed."

"Changed? You haven't changed. You stole cars and ran a chop shop before they hauled you off to treatment. Then when you break out, the first thing you do is break into Tino's car."

"This is Tino's car?" He looked like he was going to be sick.

"You ate my dog's food. *Dog* food."

He gagged.

"If Jack wasn't your uncle I'd shoot you myself."

It's hell to find a good mechanic.

"No, you wouldn't." Devin grinned. "Besides you didn't bring your gun. I can tell."

He got me. My 9mm was at home in my lingerie drawer, keeping them safe.

"We grew up together, Cat. You wouldn't whack me."

"I would whack you in a hot minute. You ruined my three-hundred dollar dress! I wore it *two hours*. And don't even get me started on my Valentino metallic stilettos!" My voice reached a near fervent pitch.

"Ha!" Devin barked. "*Three hundred dollars for a dress?* You are such a bonehead. That's a hundred-fifty ya-yos an hour."

I made a sputtering sound that would terrify small children.

He reached into the backseat and pulled out a couple bottles of soda from my surveillance cooler. He handed me one, and I hit him with it.

He laughed and rubbed his arm.

"Anyway, when I was away, I had a lot of time to think about our, uh, misunderstanding. He cleared his throat. "I wanted to say—I…uh… uhm…"

"Yes?"

"I was uh—well…"

"Come on—"

"What I am trying to say is…"

"You can't say it, can you?"

"I can say it. I'm—"

"You can do it. Spit it out, Devin."

"I'm spitting already. I'm…I'm…"

"Sor–ry." I prompted. "Just say it."

He did a mean goldfish imitation.

"Un-flipping-believable."

"Oh—just shut up and get over it, Cat!" Devin got out his flask from his inside jacket pocket and took a hefty pull.

"I don't know how far you got with the twelve steps. But you didn't stay in the program long enough for the one where you ask *forgiveness* for trying to *kill people.*"

Devin shot a sullen look. I inspected his mouth. There was a white powdery substance around his lips.

Powdered sugar.

"You got into Mama's cannoli? My God! Is nothing off limits to you?"

He opened the door. "We'll talk later. You're being a raging bitch right now. Aunt Flo must be visiting."

I lunged for him as he jumped outside laughing. I caught a flash of something in his hand.

I couldn't wrench my jaws apart. "That's my mama's Tupperware," I said through gritted teeth.

He winked. "I'll finish these off and return the container myself. I bet your mama makes me supper."

I watched as Devin disappeared into the night.

I pounded the steering wheel with my fists, took a few deep, balancing breaths. I closed my eyes and felt healing energy wash over me as I visualized slowly choking the life out of Devin.

I was ready to face my next hurdle. I punched Cleo's number on my phone.

She answered on the first ring. "Hey, girlfriend."

"So, whatcha doin'?"

"I took Cristina and Halah out to dinner, and we're on our way to a movie. Halah wants to see some weird vampire flick."

I heard Halah giggling in the background. She seemed happier now. More like a fifteen year old should be. In theory, anyway.

"You're scared of vampires, Cleo."

"And zombies. Well, all dead men walking, really." I heard her shudder.

"You should be." I laughed. "Drop the girls off at the theatre and give them cab fare. We're working tonight. We have a murder to solve."

Cleo tried to infuse regret in her voice. "Sorry to ditch ya. The Pants On Fire Detective Agency is hot on the trail of a killer!"

"We wanna come," I heard Cristina say.

Cleo's voice came back. "Cristina said—"

I cut her off. "Trust me. Cristina will be safer with the vampires."

◇◇◇

I removed a recorder from my glove box, put in the tape, and plugged in the cord from my cigarette lighter. I had one more call to make. In my business, I make a lot of these. They don't get easier.

Sylvia answered on the first ring. She had to be staring at the phone.

"Okay, Cat. What happened? Tell me all the details. And don't hold back. Please. Cat? Are you there? Hello?"

"I will tell you everything, if you will just listen," I breathed in deep. Softening my voice I continued. "I met Garrett at Bernice's Tavern. I had a little quality time with him before his friend showed up."

"Dammit, Cat, don't beat around the bush. What did he say about me? Did he show you that picture of us on the beach?"

"Uh...no."

"Did he tell you he was engaged?"

"Sylvia," I sighed. "Please just shut up for a minute and listen to me. I recorded our conversation, so you will be able to hear our whole encounter. I'll play it for you."

I heard her take a deep breath and hold it. I wondered if she'd stopped breathing.

I pressed *Play*. She was oddly quiet through the entire exchange.

"That's it," I said when it was over.

Silence.

"Sylvia, are you there?"

Her voice caught. "The caterers are gonna be pissed."

Cleo and I pushed through the Irish Pub's heavy oak doors, tromped past the bar and two other servers, and took a table in the back where the woman I remembered waited tables.

She breezed over and slapped a couple menus on the table. "I'm Katie," she said in case we couldn't read her nametag. "May I bring you ladies something from the bar?"

"I'll have a Manhattan," I said.

Snapping closed her menu, Cleo said, "A martini. And I'd like to start with an appetizer. What's good?"

"The Corned Beef Rolls are a favorite. I like the Pear and Bleu Cheese Salad. The Guinness BBQ Wings are the best I've found anywhere."

Cleo dropped the menu. "We'll take them all. I'm famished."

I waited until Katie returned with our drinks to plop my camera-purse on the table. She did a double take.

"I know that purse."

"You do," I said.

She squinted, peering closely at my face. "Same green eyes. Wow. I wouldn't have recognized you."

"Cat's incognito," Cleo blabbed. "If your boss sees her…" Cleo seized her butter knife and mock-sliced her throat.

"Smooth, Cleo," I said. "Next time, you can wait in the car with Inga."

Katie's eyes swept the room. "She's right. You do *not* want Kyle to find you here. We're supposed to tell him if we see you."

I slipped a C-note from my purse pocket. "You didn't."

She palmed it. "Ben's a good friend of mine."

"What about Cristina? Your old bartender from a few years back."

"Not so much."

"Why's that?"

"I don't like to speak ill of the dead."

"Cristina's not dead."

"The boss hasn't found her yet."

Cleo reached in my bag and dragged out another Benjamin. "Another good friend might loosen your tongue."

Katie smiled and took it saying, "You can't have too many friends. Cristina didn't work here long. She started in the kitchen, slept with the boss, next day was promoted to bartender.

"I guess you know about the shooting. The cops closed the bar for a week. We all came back except Cristina. Maybe she figured once the boss was gone, the perks she got sleeping with him were gone, too."

I shrugged. "Or maybe she left because she was traumatized by the shooting. She worked that night. It's possible she saw something."

"Cristina's a drama queen. You got that right. But she didn't work that night. She was on the schedule, but she traded shifts with another bartender."

"Liar, liar, pants on fire," Cleo said.

The server looked taken aback. "She means Cristina," I said. "Thanks for the information."

She turned to leave, then twisted around again.

"You know if my boss finds out I talked to you…"

I crossed my heart, finger-locked my lips, and threw the key away.

"Mmuaymmm," I said.

"Huh?"

"Her lips are sealed," the one with the big mouth said.

"I don't know what happened between Cristina and Kyle. But I can tell you this. The only time I've seen the boss this mad, someone was ripping him off." And Katie was gone.

We finished off the appetizers and kept the drinks coming. Cleo laughed and flirted shamelessly with a guy bussing tables.

Cleo's on a roll in the dating department. Walter, the salesman from Toledo, my crazy cousin Frankie, and the busboy. She was really reachin' for the stars.

The energy in the room shifted as I felt a hostile presence from across the room close in on me. The hair on the back of my neck rose. I tugged at my short skirt, wishing I'd worn slacks or a nun's habit. I was the gazelle, and I felt the lion salivate before I could see him coming.

I tossed down my drink and stared at my empty glass. I didn't meet his icy gaze until he plopped his butt down at our table.

"Caterina DeLuca. What an unexpected surprise."

"You're mistaken," I said, my voice disguised to a squeak.

"No." He smiled, his eyes rolling slowly over my body. "I recognized those legs when you walked in my door. They're a work of art."

"The better to kick you with," I snarled.

He smiled, amused.

"What are you doing here, Cat?"

"I'm investigating your sorry ass, Kyle Tierney. I'm gathering evidence. You killed Billy Bonham and you're not getting away with it."

A chill seeped into his face and his voice was dangerously soft. "If you were a man, I'd have dealt with you long ago."

"Like you dealt with Billy Bonham?" Cleo piped in.

Tierney looked at her as if seeing her for the first time. "I know you from somewhere. You danced at one of my clubs, didn't you?"

"She did not!" I elbow-slugged her. "*Did you?*"

He glanced down at her legs. "My mistake."

"You're a pig, Tierney," I said.

"These are *fabulous* legs," Cleo snapped. "They could dance the shit out of your sleazy night clubs."

He snapped his fingers and aimed his pointy finger at Cleo. "Got it! You're the crazy woman on the video. You whacked your husband last summer."

Her face twitched. I slapped a hand on her bag before she threw herself over the table and smacked him with it.

"The charges against Cleo were dropped," I said.

"*Right.*" He winked.

He held up a hand and wriggled a finger. One of his stooges fell over himself sprinting over. "Sir?"

"Bring these women a bottle of Jameson Whiskey from my personal collection."

He scooted away and Tierney flashed a cool smile. "You see? I'm not the monster you think I am."

"Satan?" I said.

His jaw tightened. "Enjoy your meal, ladies. It's on me."

Cleo couldn't help herself. She loves free food. "Wow," she said. "Thanks."

I elbowed slugged her again.

"At least I'm not crazy enough to kill Santa," she called after him.

Tierney twisted around to look at her. This time the smile reached his eyes.

"You can't kill Santa Claus, Ms. Jones. Everybody knows that."

◇◇◇

Tierney's free food and booze was too much for Cleo to resist. She staggered from the pub groaning, vowing she'd never eat again. I shoved her into Tino's Buick, ditched the wig, and cranked up the engine. Cleo's declaration lasted as long as it took to cruise to Tino's Deli. Five minutes.

Max and Tino were locked in battle over a chess board as we came through the door, Cleo steadying herself a bit on my arm.

Max took in the dress I wore to seduce Sylvia's fiancé and his golden eyes smiled. "God you're beautiful."

"Schank-you," Cleo sniffed. "That pig Tierney didn't appsheeate theese legsh."

Max frowned. "You were at his pub?"

"In disguise," I said pointedly.

"And Tierney didn't recognize you?"

"He knew her legsh right off," Cleo blabbed.

"As would I," the sausage maker said returning with two strong coffees and a plate of ricciarelli cookies.

Cleo's eyes got wide. "Yummy," she said and made a dive for the cookies.

Tino cleared his throat, "I asked around about the dead guy in Tierney's bar. His name was Alan Mitchell. Age twenty-seven. No criminal record. No obvious ties to Tierney. Tierney claimed Mitchell broke into the bar after hours to rob him. There was no weapon and no signs of a break-in to support his story."

"Kyle Tierney is a big, fat liar," I said.

"He's not the only one." Tino said. "Cristina and Alan Mitchell lived in the same three-story walk-up on the North Side. There's no way they didn't know each other."

"Imagine that," Cleo said.

"I'll kill her," I said.

Max said, "The question is, did her lies get Billy killed?"

"I'll double kill her," I said.

"There's something else," Tino said. "The night Alan Mitchell died, the Palmer House Hilton Hotel downtown hosted a political fund-raiser. A bunch of Hollywood actors were there."

"George Clooney?" I said.

Tino nodded.

"Damn," I said.

"Women say I look like George Clooney." Max grinned.

Cleo stared at Max, her eyes slits. "I can shee it if I schquint. Try it, Cat."

"*Seriously?*"

Tino swallowed a smile. "The fundraiser event sold one hundred dinner tickets at ten grand each."

Cleo feigned a whistle. "That's a whole lot of pashta."

"There was even more jewelry," Tino said. "Ten thousand dollars bought you a photo op with the stars *and* a close and personal look at some Hollywood history. Original pieces worn by Marilyn Monroe in *Some Like It Hot* and in *Gentlemen Prefer Blondes* were on display."

Max said, "Tino has a crush on Marilyn."

"What man doesn't?" Tino said. He topped our coffees. "The theft wasn't discovered until the following morning."

"What was missing?"

"Marilyn's diamond earrings from *Some Like It Hot*. They had been replaced with a replica."

"The value?"

"An auction would bring millions. The earrings were a favorite of Marilyn's. She had the original Hollywood glass replaced with real diamonds. She wore the earrings at a dinner party in the White House. The studio and insurance company both offered fat rewards. The earrings were never found."

"So what's this have to do with Alan Mitchell?" I said.

Tino leaned close, his dark eyes gleaming. "Maybe nothing. But there are four million people in Chicago. The night Marilyn's diamonds disappeared, one *hundred* of those people paid ten thousand dollars each to dine with the stars. And Alan Mitchell—a guy between jobs, maxed on his credit cards and living in a crappy apartment—was one of them."

My breath caught. "Are you sure?"

Tino smiled. "The ticket was in his pocket. And George Clooney signed it for him."

Chapter Eighteen

The doorbell woke me just before seven. I pulled the pillow over my head. It was way too early for good news. And I'd had enough of the bad stuff lately. I didn't know who was out there, but it couldn't be a member of my family.

I know this because I have a premium platinum alarm system. My brother Rocco had it installed last summer after someone left a dead rat in my bed. It's kept the rats out since. But DeLucas are a plethora of cops and crooks. They trample past my security like it's a revolving door at Macy's.

The bell rang again. I wiggled into my bunny slippers and grumbled all the way to the door. Anyone cruel enough to show up before my first cup of coffee had best be bringing donuts.

I flung open the door and Mrs. Bonham attempted an apologetic smile. She removed her sunglasses. They were the wrap-around type with dark frames. She wore them to conceal red, swollen eyes. God knows the sun was barely up.

I scanned her hands for a white bag. No donuts, dammit.

"I hope I'm not intruding."

Tying my robe, I said, "Not at all. Come in. I'll make coffee."

She followed me to the kitchen.

"I would have called—"

"Calling is good."

"—but I didn't have your number. And I didn't want to wake your mother."

I smiled. "By now she's made Papa's breakfast, taken my dog for a walk, and is probably pulling bruschetta from the oven."

"Your mama is a wonder."

"Yeah. I wonder about her too."

I ground the darkest beans I had, and made a thick, caffeine-rich sludge in my French Press.

In lieu of donuts, I ducked my head in the fridge. I suspected it was a little early to break out the chocolate fudge cake. I thought I deserved it. Being dragged out of bed by a woman crying at your door is a scream for chocolate.

I dipped my finger into the fudge frosting and popped out of the fridge with a bowl of grapes and my extra Tupperware of Mama's pastries.

I sat with Mrs. Bonham. She dumped cream in her coffee and two sugar cubes.

"Have you caught the killer, dear?"

"Not yet, but I have pulled every available resource I have to help me on this. With a couple of cops, the FBI, and two ex-spies, we'll follow the evidence and see where it takes us."

The fact was, there was an astounding lack of evidence to follow.

Mrs. Bonham nodded soberly.

"I can't really talk about the investigation, but I can tell you we have a prime suspect."

"What does Captain Bob say?"

"Bob is on, let's just say, a different page."

Mrs. Bonham nodded. "I don't think he liked my son all that much."

"Really? I can't imagine why."

She bit her lip worriedly. "I'm afraid you'll be in hot water with the captain."

"I wouldn't worry all that much." I laughed. "Billy would get a kick out of that."

She smiled.

"Why are you here, Mrs. Bonham?"

Her brow furrowed. "Well, someone was in my house yesterday. They broke in when I was at the funeral home making arrangements."

"Did you call the police?"

She shook her head. "I didn't notice until last night. I couldn't sleep so I went into Billy's room. A few things had been moved around. Most people wouldn't see it. But I'm a fastidious housekeeper."

Billy had called her anal-retentive.

Mrs. Bonham glanced around my kitchen with unspoken approval. I silently blessed the Merry Maids. They had been here yesterday.

"Do you have any ideas of who it could have been?" I said.

"It was Nicole. I'm sure of it."

"Ah. Billy's ex."

"Not ex, dear. There wasn't a divorce yet. Billy was hurt she left him. He went on bragging about a big payment he was expecting from a client. Something about diamonds. It was nothing but a hot-air. Billy, God love him, was a blowhard. Like his old man."

I figured the "big payment" was the mother lode of cash Billy expected to find in Kyle Tierney's safe.

"I'd like to talk to Nicole. Do you know where she'd be staying? Does she have friends here?"

"If she has half a brain, she's gone back home."

"To Kansas."

Mrs. Bonham gave an odd smile. "I was thinking, Oz."

We finished off two pots of coffee and all the pastries. I gave her my card, and she put my number in her phone.

I had a caffeine buzz when we walked to the porch.

"Billy loved you," his mama said. "The night he died, he told me you were the one who got away."

I laughed. "Billy had been drinking."

I watched her drive away and took a long, steamy shower. I blow-dried my hair and threw on my fav pair of black curvy jeans and a soft peach sweater. When I finished, doing my five minute make-up routine, a message was waiting on my phone.

It was from Mrs. Bonham.

"Caterina, I meant to ask if Billy mentioned something about his St. Christopher necklace. You'll remember it. I bought it for his Confirmation. Captain Bob insists it wasn't found on him. I never saw Billy without it." Her voice caught. "I don't want to bury him without his St. Christopher necklace."

She shouldn't have to. She's had enough grief already. The funeral was in two days. I didn't have a lot of time.

I stepped into a pair of black wedge booties, grabbed my slate jacket, slung my Tignanello tote over my shoulder, and headed for the door.

I had a plan. I was pretty sure I knew where Billy's St. Christopher was. He lost it to a pair of aces.

◇◇◇

Before my hand found the knob, the door pushed open. Uncle Joey stood on the porch, a large box in his arms. Four more boxes were stacked beside him.

I said, "Did you ever know that you're my hero?"

Uncle Joey grinned. "Everything we know about the life and death of Alan Mitchell is in these boxes."

"It looks like a lot."

"I flipped through them last night. I can cut to the chase and give you the condensed version."

"Cut away."

"Alan Mitchell is dead."

I kissed my uncle's cheek and hoisted a box in my arms. "Come in. I'll make coffee."

My Uncle Joey is a Chicago cop in the true DeLuca family tradition. He, however, does it better than most. He lives in a big house with a swimming pool. And he lives large. Joey rubs elbows with some of the most powerful men in Chicago. He also knows where their secrets are buried. He's generous and fiercely loyal to his family and friends. I'm not saying my uncle's in anybody's pocket. But I suspect he has his hand in more than one cookie jar.

We set the boxes around the kitchen table. I made coffee while Uncle Joey noshed on some beef curry pillows Cleo made for Mrs. Millani's bridge party.

I nosed through a box. I found crime photos and my chest tightened. There were detectives' notes from interviews with the victim's family and friends. The investigators couldn't establish a connection between Mitchell and Tierney. The staff did not remember serving him at the pub.

Uncle Joey said, "Tierney claimed it was a robbery gone wrong. Mitchell tried to rob him. But the only gun in the room was Tierney's. And he shot Mitchell with it."

"What do you think?"

Uncle Joey seized a garlic-drowned shrimp. "I think if a cop hadn't heard the shot, Mitchell's body would be on the bottom of the lake wrapped in chains."

Uncle Joey added, "The night he died, Mitchell told friends he was performing a magic act for a Boys Club in Skokie."

"Why lie?"

Joey shrugged. "The Boy's Club date was a month out."

"He's not the only one who lied. Cristina told Billy she tended bar that night. She didn't. She got someone else to cover her shift."

"Interesting."

"Oh, and you'll love this. Tino says Cristina and Mitchell knew each other."

His eyebrows shot up. "Knew each other?"

Uncle Joey stretched back in his chair and rubbed his stomach. "Okay, so it appears the connection between Mitchell and Tierney was the bartender."

I walked over to the coffee pot and refilled his mug. "The night Mitchell was killed, he attended a political fundraiser at the Palmer House Hilton Hotel. Tickets went for ten grand each."

Joey snorted. "That's half of Mitchell's earnings for the year."

"It gets better. The event showed off celebrities and Hollywood jewelry. A pair of Marilyn Monroe's diamond earrings went missing that night. They were never found."

A slow smile spread across Uncle Joey's face.

I said, "Alan was a magician. He could pull rabbits out of a hat, coins out of children's ears, and handkerchiefs out of hands."

"He could make earrings disappear."

Uncle Joey dragged another box onto the table. He removed the lid and stuffed a hand inside. He opened a small plastic bag and pulled out a pair of chandelier earrings made with round, cascading crystals.

"These earrings were at the crime scene. Costume jewelry. They were close enough to the body to be bagged with the evidence."

"Oh my God."

He peered closely at the earrings. "What?"

I zipped to the bedroom and returned with my laptop. Joey scooted his chair next to mine. Moments later I had the newspaper article up.

The headline, Marilyn's Diamonds Stolen from Star Studded Fundraiser, filled the screen. I looked at the earrings on my computer screen. And I stared at the glass copies in my hands.

My heart skipped around in my chest. I couldn't breathe.

A slow chortle began in Uncle Joey's throat and swelled to a full-out *bwahahaha* belly laugh.

Other than a ten million dollar price difference, they were identical.

Chapter Nineteen

When Uncle Joey was gone, I sat in the kitchen with the earrings and the crime scene photos. Alan Mitchell was dressed in the usual black tie fundraiser garb. Not designer label, but decent quality. An ugly brown-red stain covered most of Alan Mitchell's white shirt. He'd taken a hit in the chest that propelled him backwards. He lay sprawled on his back, legs twisted as if they'd crumbled beneath him. The earrings aligned with an outstretched hand.

There were no visible signs of struggle. Chairs were in place. Tierney's glass and the bottle of Jameson remained undisturbed on the table. Not a drop had been spilled in the violent exchange that ended Mitchell's life.

I brushed the crumbs from the table and piled our dishes in the dishwasher. I grabbed my Alfani slate-colored jacket and Tignanello tote again.

I stepped outside and locked the door behind me. I beeped the alarm on Tino's Buick.

Half way down my steps, there was a sound. A horrible sound that mimicked fingernails on chalkboard came drifting around the side of my house.

"Hey! Open up."

I winced. "Sylvia?"

The red-head flounced around and met me at the front. I was relieved she left her fox friends behind.

"I had to look up your website," she said. "Your address wasn't on your card."

"My address isn't on my website, either."

She sniffed disapprovingly. "I don't know how you expect to get business."

The omission of my address isn't an oversight. I piss off too many people to hang out a welcome mat. Especially with my office attached to my home. I get enough uninvited guests as it is.

I heard my teeth grind. "You apparently skipped the part about calling for an appointment."

She shrugged. "I saw it."

I forced the edges of my mouth to curve. "Well then how'd you find me?"

"What can I say? I've got the gift."

"Like a stalker." I unlocked the door. "There should be a cup left in the pot. Come on in."

Sylvia followed me to the kitchen, and I poured her a mug of coffee.

"Eeeuw!" she said standing over the crime photos. "Is that guy dead?"

"Deader than Elvis."

I shuffled the pictures into a pile and put them back in the box. "This is for a case I'm working on."

Sylvia twirled the earrings in her hand. "Are these real?"

"They're copies of the real ones." I scooped them from her palm, tossed them in the box, and dropped the box on the floor with the others.

Sylvia plopped on a chair and leaned forward. Her boobs, and the butterfly tattoo, nearly spilled out on the table. She gave a conspiratorial wink.

"Whatcha gonna do when you find the real ones?"

I massaged my temples. "What makes you think I'm looking for the real diamonds."

"Well duh! You're a detective, aren't cha?"

"Sylvia," I said, now rubbing my temples. "Why did you want to see me?"

"I need to use your can."

Lovely. "It's down the—"

She waved a hand. "Yeah, yeah. I know. I saw it when I came in."

She trotted off and I downed a glass of water with a couple Excedrin. Sylvia was going through a rough time, I told myself. She'd been played by the man she loved. Her wedding was off. The gossip vultures that she called friends would be circling. In time, if she's smart, she would be doing the happy dance. Sylvia was lucky to get out before she had to split her hard-earned grieving cash with that money whore.

She emerged from the bathroom with tears in her eyes.

"What's going on, Sylvia?"

She pressed her lips together. "Garret is a madman. He's pissed I cancelled the wedding, and I don't know what he'll do."

"Has he threatened you in any way?"

"I'd kick his ass. But he spilled red wine on my white carpet for God's sake. The man is a maniac. Who knows what he will do next."

"I know this is hard. But you'll get through this."

"You're the one who told me not to marry him. This is all your fault. I didn't know who else to turn to."

"I—what?"

Sylvia blew her nose hard, fully activating the fog horn.

"The man was built like a god. Not that Howie was a slouch, mind you."

"Okay. But for the record, I did not…"

"But Garret was a gorgeous hunk of man meat. I know someday he'll get over me. He'll forget me and find someone else."

Her words threw her in torrential sobs.

"I am sure you are right." From what I'd seen and heard of Garret Swearingen, forgetting and finding wouldn't be a problem.

"I mean, my God, Cat, you practically entrapped the poor man."

I went to my office for another box of tissues and fought the urge to duck out the door. I whispered a few choice words to Billy, trudged back to the kitchen, and waited for Sylvia to pull it together.

She sniffed. "You—you never gave Garrett a chance. You were against him from the start."

I opened my mouth and no sound came out.

In a blink her eyes were dry and she regarded me with distaste. "Don't you dare bill me for your services. I paid Billy in full."

"I understand."

"Bill was supposed to handle my case. I've a good mind to stop payment on my check."

If I knew Billy, he dashed to the bank before the ink was dry. I said, "Good luck with that."

Sylvia slapped her hands on the table and rose to her feet. She leaned in toward me. I felt her coffee breath on my face.

"What Garrett and I had was special. We understood each other. But a woman like you, Cat DeLuca, will always be alone."

Whack-job!

My head did a double-take and my eyes flashed on the boobs in my face. I pulled back and wagged a finger left and then right.

"Wasn't that butterfly on the other boob yesterday?"

Sylvia snorted. "Tattoos don't fly, Cat. Everybody knows that."

Chapter Twenty

The first boy I kissed was a vampire. His pasty face gave me a white mustache but I didn't care. I was a warrior princess and I was wearing the shit out of Mama's make-up.

It was Halloween night. For two whole hours our south-side gang owned the streets of Bridgeport. When our sacks got heavy, Billy and I hung back and shone a flashlight in our bags.

There was soooo much candy.

That's when he kissed me. Billy couldn't help himself. He loved candy.

The wax vampire fangs tickled my mouth. The quick, full-on smooch tasted like cinnamon.

Billy Bonham was delicious.

"You're going to marry me someday, Cat DeLuca," he said.

We were eight.

Billy told me the women who beat him in strip poker lived across the street from the ghost house.

He was talking about a Halloween night when vampires and ninjas ruled the streets. It was the first year Mama didn't hover over us from the sidewalk. We took down Bridgeport block after block until our bags bulged, and we were tired and cold.

"My taffeta is scratchy," Sophie said. "I want to go home.

My switched-at-birth sister was the only glittery-pink princess in our South Chicago gang that year.

I checked my bag. I had enough Jawbreakers and Jolly Ranchers to seriously bond with my dentist and his torture devices.

"I'm ready," I said.

The others agreed. Billy was the last holdout. He screwed up his face and crossed his arms across his chest.

"I ain't got no Hot Tamales," he said.

"We all got red hots," Rocco said.

Rocco beamed his flashlight on Billy's face. His lips were red. He sniffed. *Cinnamon.*

Rocco frowned. "You ate the Hot Tamales. You're supposed to wait until your Papa checks it."

"I ain't afraid of no razor blades."

Rocco signaled the gang. "We're going home."

Billy's gaze cut to the next house. It was dark and spooky. I was pretty sure Jason Vorhees was waiting for us inside the door.

Billy flapped his vampire cape. He howled. "One more score!"

I shuddered. "Not that house. It's…creepy."

"It's Halloween, you big chickens!"

I called to my brother, "Rocco, wait! We're supposed to stick together."

I turned back and the blood-sucking vampire was gone. I tore after him.

"Stop, Billy. I don't like it here."

"Cluck cluck cluck!" He tromped up the dark steps and banged on the door.

I caught up on the porch and tugged at his sleeve. "Nobody's home."

"There's a light on in back."

"If they're home, they're outta candy. And I'm pretty sure they eat kids."

I felt my stomach clench. There was the sound of bushes parting and a zombie emerged from the shadows. He did the creepy death that known zombies do—their outstretched arms devour small children.

We screamed. My legs turned to cement. Not Billy's. He was all about saving the candy. Boots pounded the pavement and Billy jetted past the others. He didn't stop until he was home.

Billy didn't hear the old man laughing. Or his wife scold him from the porch.

The old woman wrapped two fat slices of pumpkin bread and added them to my bag. There were chocolate chips and yellow raisins. And they were still warm.

A big brown bear in a Chicago football jersey waited for me down the block.

"Are you okay, Sis?" Rocco said.

My brother flashed a light and growled at the white face-paint mustache where Billy kissed me. Rocco didn't leave me alone with Billy Bonham after that.

I saved a slice of pumpkin bread for Billy. I never had the heart to tell him where it came from.

I smiled at the memory and pulled Tino's car in front of the pumpkin bread house. It had a fresh coat of paint. The old man and old woman would be long gone. But the street hadn't changed much since we were kids. People move away. Young families replace some of the faces we knew. Other people stay. Like my parents.

Mama's feet are firmly entrenched in Bridgeport. She plans to die surrounded by her grandchildren. She says if I want her to die happy, I'll call Father Timothy and reserve the church.

"You should marry that nice FBI agent," Mama says. "The one with good insurance. I can't promise your Aunt Francesca will be there. Not after the FBI snubbed your cousin Frankie. But at your age…"

Mama's eyes drag to the grandfather clock her papa brought over from Italy.

Tick tock.

I studied four houses across the street. Billy's St. Christopher necklace had to be inside one of them. A. B. C. Or D. And if it wasn't, the women who conned Billy would know where it was.

I moved the plush leather seat back, kicked off my shoes, and opened the latest Laura Caldwell novel. Izzy McNeil is my kind of woman. She's Chicago tough. Street smart. And she always gets her man.

A short fifteen minutes passed and a muted blue Nissan Altima pulled up in front of House C. I watched the suit get out of his car, enter the house, and turn on lights. He was followed ten minutes later by a second suit bearing a key and bearing Chinese Takeout. I whipped out my binoculars. My gaydar screamed before he made it to the door. The men kissed briefly and sat at the table. I took House C off my list, put away my spy eyes, and made a mental note to order Chinese food for dinner.

I opened my surveillance cooler and sliced up an apple. I smelled Inga's sausages. I missed my partner.

I eliminated House A before I finished my apple. Mom came home in a minivan with three kids under five and four bags of groceries. I couldn't imagine her having the energy to seduce Billy or ever wanting to see him naked.

That left houses B and D. I flipped a coin and went with B. The morning paper was still on the porch. They either left early, before it was delivered, didn't come home last night, or hadn't stepped onto the porch today.

At least I could scratch one possibility off my list. I checked the mirror and wiped a smudge of mascara from under my eye. I wet my lips with Dr. Pepper Lip Smacker.

Crossing the street, my eye caught a window on the side of the house. The screen was off, propped against the building. My heartbeat quickened. I'd found the house. And the window the women pushed Billy out of. I jabbed a hand in my pocket and fingered my lock picks. If no one answered, I had my own keys. I would be going in.

The door was new. Big, expensive, and possibly reinforced with steel. More than enough to keep a guy like Billy from kicking it down to recover his stuff. The lock was a Masterlock. Not impossible to pick but a little tricky.

I climbed the steps and a voice shouted over the whirr of a vacuum cleaner.

"Shut it off, babe. I'm talkin' on the phone here."

Cheery.

The vacuum stopped and I rang the bell. No answer. I pounded the door with my fist and rang again. The door opened a crack, revealing half a face. The chain was on.

"We don't want nothing you're selling," the blond said. "So get off my property."

Charming.

"I'm here for Bill. Remember him? The guy you screwed over."

"Listen you psycho bitch, I don't know who you're talking about, but—"

"I am not here for an argument. I only care about his St. Christopher necklace. You can keep the rest."

"Leave now," she said in an eerily calm voice.

She started to slam the door in my face and I blocked it with my foot.

"Look," I said with as much politeness as I could muster. "Just give me the necklace. I'll go away, no questions asked. You'll never hear from me again."

A big tough-looking ogre sporting a gold tooth came to the door. "You heard the lady. Bounce."

"Look, I get it. He was drunk and an easy score." I batted my eyelashes. "All I am asking for is a lame St. Christopher's medal that has sentimental meaning to the family. You can give me that, can't you?"

He stared at me like I spoke Klingon. "Yo, little lady, I got no beef with ya's. It's like she says. We don't know what you's are talkin' bout."

I smiled, and breathed. "Okay, well it was worth a shot. My friend was so wasted he had no idea where he was. I've been up and down these blocks. I've struck out a dozen times. I give up."

"Just go buy his mom another St. Christopher necklace. She won't know da difference, ya know?"

The blond stood behind him, eyes focused. "See, now that's a good idea."

"What a fabulous idea!" I did the head conk thing with my hand. "Why didn't I think of that? Okay well, sorry to bother you," I said doing my best parade wave, as I scooted my butt to Tino's Buick feeling their eyes on my back. I dropped my head on the steering wheel and breathed a huge sigh as soon as I heard the front door slam.

Oh, I will be back.

Chapter Twenty-one

My pocket vibrated before I could start the engine. It was my brother.

"Yo," Rocco said. "The results came back on Cristina *Lindstrom's* fingerprints."

"What happened to McTigue?"

He laughed. "She's full of surprises. I hope you're at your computer. I'm pushing send now."

I picked up Rocco's email on my phone. Then I called Cristina. Halah answered.

"Whatcha doin?" I asked.

"Lunch."

"Where?"

"Connie's Restaurant."

I cranked the engine. "I'm on my way."

Five minutes later I pulled up a chair beside Halah and snagged a fry.

"Hey," she whined.

"Your mom and I need to step outside for a minute. When the server comes by, order me a Mediterranean Chicken Salad. And a Pepsi."

"Okay. But you're getting your own fries."

"They won't taste as good as yours."

Cristina grabbed her jacket and followed me. "What's happening? Are you ready to crack the case?"

"I'm ready to crack your head. You lied to me, Cristina *Lindstrom*."

She huffed with indignation. "You investigated me? How rude is that?"

"Ten years ago you were arrested for petty theft. You stole your employer's piggybank."

"Some people just can't take a joke."

"There was three thousand dollars in it." I blew a sigh. "Eight years ago you did forty days in a Cincinnati jail for pawning a gold cross that was stolen from a church rectory."

"I found it."

"In the *rectory*. You pissed off God."

"I went to Confession."

"*Seriously?* Have you no *shame?*" I sounded like my mother.

Cristina Lindstrom waved a hand, blowing me off. She was clearly raised by wolves.

"That's why Tierney left a note in his safe. He knew you were a thief. He figured you'd come around for the cash."

Her eyes flickered slightly.

"Why didn't you tell Billy that Tierney was your lover?"

"Do you always blab who you slept with?"

"Depends if I am asking for help."

She shrugged. "Whatever."

"You lied to Billy about Marilyn's diamond."

The doe eyes widened. "Oops."

"Oh yeah. I'm onto you, girlfriend. Alan Mitchell was your partner. He stole Marilyn's diamond earrings from the Palmer House Hilton the night your boyfriend killed him. You were up to your eyeballs in the heist. What I don't know is how Kyle Tierney fits in."

She blew off the question.

"Kyle dumped me. He moved on."

"But you didn't. You wanted revenge."

She smiled a slow sardonic grin. "Some like it hot."

"So if Tierney doesn't have the diamonds—"

"Kyle's a liar."

I had to give her that. "But he's not lying about this. So where are they?"

"You figure it out. You're the hotshot detective."

She did a little pouty thing with her mouth. "You're still going to help me, right?"

"Wrong."

"That's it? That's all you have to say?"

"No. I have another word for you. Therapy. Get some."

"So you're gonna walk away? Tierney gets by with killing Billy."

"Oh, I'm getting Tierney. Without you. You're heading home to California tomorrow."

"I'm not leaving. You're stuck with me. I don't care about the diamonds anymore. I'm here to get Tierney. I owe it to Billy."

"Really?"

"I swear on my mother's grave."

"Is your mother even dead?" A thought came to me. "Oh my God! You're not really dying, are you."

"We're all dying," she snapped and then almost looked sheepish. "I know. It was a terrible thing to say. But Billy wasn't going to take my case. Two other investigators already turned me down. Once Billy thought I was dying, he was all over it."

"You have no soul."

"Now that's plain silly." She laughed and took my arm. "My lunch is getting cold. And next time don't drag me outside. I don't keep secrets from my daughter. I tell her everything."

"Poor kid," I said, and held the door for her.

Chapter Twenty-two

The woman is certifiable. But I learned a long time ago you can't kill people who make you crazy. If you could, I'd be an orphan.

I left Connie's and drove straight to LA Fitness. Working out makes me feel better than Ding Dongs. And it's cheaper than therapy. I worked the machines and did laps in the pool until I wasn't irritated any longer. Cristina was hard to shake. It took twenty extra laps and an ice cream cone at Scoops on my way home.

There was a message on my phone when I returned from the gym. The voice was timid.

"Uh, Cat? This is Brenda Greger. You may not remember me."

Oh. I remembered.

"I hired you last summer to follow my husband, Steve."

Toothy boy.

"I thought Steve was cheating on me."

He was.

"I don't know why I let him convince me otherwise."

Cuz you're a kind fool with jelly for a backbone.

"Steve's out again tonight. He says he's working late. I know he's with *her*. She wears Amazing Grace perfume."

That would be the tall blond woman I call Legs.

"I don't know who else to turn to. You have my number."

I dialed it. The call went to voice-mail.

"Brenda, this is Cat. Call ONSTAR and have them tell you where Steve's car is. We finish this tonight."

I parked on Clark behind Steve's beemer and studied the row of apartments. All were two- and three-story walk-ups. I had a hunch Legs lived in one of them.

I freshened my Dr. Pepper Lip Gloss in the visor mirror. A curly grey wig, cane, a lilac-flowered polyester dress, and a mauve-colored pin hat with a fine netting that covered half my face and a pair of cat-rimmed glasses. I hardly recognized myself. Toothy Boy sure as hell wouldn't.

I chased the cheater and his girlfriend last summer. He took her to his love boat at the marina. I caught them in bed, her platform shoes saluting the ceiling. It was a classic Kodak-moment, and I missed my shot. Steve was onto me after that. Toying, taunting. Flashing his blinding, toothy-white smile. He schmoozed his wife and she fired me. I bided my time and waited for her to call. PI Cat DeLuca always gets her cheater.

I readied my camera, lowered my window, and hurled a tennis ball at Steve Greger's car. The car-alarm wailed, lights flashed. Steve appeared in a doorway and scuttled down the steps. His shirt was unbuttoned, and he forgot his shoes.

Another Kodak moment. *Click.*

An upstairs curtain moved and Legs hid behind it. Not well. *Click.* She forgot her clothes.

Steve silenced the alarm. He walked around the car, checking for damage. His shoulders lost their tension. He probably decided a cat lit on his hood. And then he saw the old woman parked behind him. He glared at me and felt his hand along the bumper. Maybe he found a nick he hadn't noticed before. Cuz he stiffened and marched over to Tino's car.

He rapped on the glass and made circles with his index finger. I unrolled the window and squinted through the glare of his incredibly large white teeth.

"What?" I croaked.

"Ma'am, did you hit my car?"

I cupped my ear. "Did you say you hit my car?"

"*You* hit *my* car," and added "you crazy old bat" under his breath.

"Fat?!!" I whipped out my cell. "I'm calling the police."

"No!" He lunged for the phone. I stashed it in my bra.

"Pervert!" I croaked and slammed on my horn.

The last thing Steve Greger wanted was Brenda to know where he put in his overtime.

Too late, toothy boy.

I snatched my cane and hit him with it.

I parked the Buick farther down the street where it couldn't be seen from Legs' window. Peeling off the old lady digs, I slipped outside in the jeans I wore beneath the frumpy dress.

The building was a three-story triplex. The tenants in the basement apartment had kids. Their bikes were chained to the back porch, finger paintings taped to the windows. My mark was in the apartment above them. Clinging to the shadows, I made my way around the building and stopped below the window with a bluish flickering light from a TV. I'd found the bedroom.

I looked around for a way up. The rusted, creaky fire-escape would be as subtle as a three alarm fire. I focused on the tree. The oak was off center but climbing out on a branch would give me a decent shot. I hoisted a leg up. And then I saw the rope swing.

Gotta love a house with kids.

The swing was a single rope, knotted at the base to support a wooden, donut-shaped seat. I pushed up the seat and tied a knot two feet higher on the rope. Then I climbed onto the seat, got to my feet, and swung. Clumsy at first, testing my balance. Gaining height and momentum with each sweep of the rope. I could fly like a bird.

They were in bed. *The Daily Show* was on the television, but they were missing Jon Stewart's good jokes. I swooped by again and again. While clinging to the rope with one hand, and extending a small digital camera in the other. A perfect shot with each sweep.

Hello. *Click.* Good-bye.

Legs saw me first. *Click.* She let out a little scream. When toothy-boy looked up, the angel of Karma was gone.

Legs was stiff and wide-eyed when I breezed past again. I waved my pinky. *Say cheese.*

She screamed. I was gone again.

On my final fly-by, Steve stood at the window, watching—with horror—his rich wife's money fly away. Legs hovered behind him. He covered himself with her pink bikini panties. As if I hadn't seen it all before. Trust me, a thong would have been enough.

Click.

"Gotcha," I said.

Brenda's kids were doing homework when I dropped by her house.

"I'm sorry," I said, and handed over the 8x10 glossies.

She stared at the envelope in her hand. "I guess I've always known. I just didn't want to admit it."

"Would you like me to stay?"

"My sister's on her way." She gave a sad smile. "Thanks for not giving up on me."

I drove straight home and swung by the kitchen long enough to uncork a bottle of wine and snag a glass.

My hands had rope burns, and I was smudged with the kind of dirty, sticky goo trees give off. I drew a hot bubble bath. I dropped my clothes on the floor slid into the tub beneath the sweet smelling bubbles.

I turned on the jets and might have dozed off when a door slammed. A Cleo-sized screech pierced the air. I breathed again.

"Cat! Are you here?"

"No! Go away."

Cleo laughed and poked her head in the bathroom. The woman has no boundaries.

"Whatcha doin?'"

"*Seriously?*"

Halah popped her head in. "Awesome bubbles!"

"Uh, naked here," I said.

Cristina shoved the others aside. "What's your order, girl-friend? The bartender is in."

The pepper-spray princess smiled broadly. "It's a party, Cat."

I realized I would miss her. And if God had any compassion, this would be our last night together. Tomorrow the duo would point the nose of their Subaru west. And drive.

The thought made me giddy.

I spoke as soberly as I could through a full-on grin. "A cucumber mojito, bartender. Let's get this farewell party started."

"They're not going anywhere," Cleo said.

I threw her a look. "Don't pop my bubbles."

Cristina waved a floppy hand. "There is no way that Subaru makes it to California. We got here on black smoke and fumes."

"Halah has school, for God sake. I'll help you. Train? Plane? Buckshot?"

"You're such a kidder," Cleo laughed. "We're a team."

"No. We're not," I said doing a circling motion with my bubble-laden fingers.

"The four of us are hot on the trail of a killer, and no one leaves until Billy's death is avenged." Cleo waggled her hand in the air with meaning.

The three high-fived. I could've pushed past my bubbles and taken them all down.

Instead I said, "Cristina's done too much already."

I suspected her fibs put a bulls-eye on Billy's chest. I was certain Cristina never intended to harm Billy. Yes, her actions were selfish and manipulative. But she wasn't the one that pulled the trigger. If my suspicions were right, I hoped she'd never connect the dots. It would be a terrible truth to live with.

I shooed them away and watched my bubbles disappear down the drain.

I dressed in yoga sweats for my night run and slicked my hair back in a ponytail. A flash of gold on the dresser caught my eye. I scooped up the cigarette lighter to stash in my surveillance box. Then I padded to the living room where my cucumber mojito was waiting for me.

I took a sip and my eyes rolled back in my head. "This is the *best* mojito I've ever tasted."

Cleo's eyes didn't blink from the game of Checkers she was playing with Halah. She said, "That's a real compliment. God knows she's tasted a lot."

Cristina plunked beside me on the couch. "So what's going on with you and Max?"

I gulped my drink. "What?"

"Are you blind? The guy is a serious hottie bom botty. If you're not hitting that, I'm going for him."

She wet her lips and her eyes lowered to slits. Her tongue brushed across her teeth. She was going in for the kill.

"You should play nice," I said. "Max is a great guy."

"What is that supposed to mean?"

"Your last affair in Bridgeport ended badly." *Things didn't end so well for Billy either.*

She shrugged. "Love and war. Don't worry about Max. He's a big boy. I am sure he can take care of himself."

My hands were creeping up dangerously close to her neck. I slid them behind my back. "You still don't get it. Mitchell was *murdered*. Tierney *went to prison.*"

"Yeah he did. And I felt really bad about that. I went to Confession and everything."

"You spend a lot of time in that booth?"

She sniffed. "Max and I have chemistry. I'm calling him tonight."

"Go for it. But I should warn you, Tino is Max's best friend. You don't want to screw him over like you screwed Kyle."

She tilted her head and smiled. "Why should Tino care?"

I smiled back. "Because Tino is the guy I'll get to kill you."

Her eyes went blink blink. "You're hilarious."

◇◇◇

Halah put on a Chicago Symphony CD that Cleo had bought her, and played along with her violin. Inga and Cleo's black Tibetan Terrier fought over a big rubber Kong toy. They twisted and tangled and turned into the standing lamp cord until it crashed across the floor. Chasing the dogs outside, I grabbed the broom.

Cleo was making cheesy crab appetizers and cutting up raw veggies while Cristina served up drinks. Another round of cucumber mojitos and a virgin mojito for her daughter.

"Keep the drinks coming," Cleo said. "This mojito is like drinking a salad. I'm getting a healthy serving of vegetables right here."

Cristina said, "I left a message on Max's phone. I told him to call me."

"Do you have time for a run?" I said.

Her face lit. "Always."

I glanced at Cleo. She worked her eyes back and forth, searching for any excuse. My assistant spends more energy than anyone I know avoiding exercise.

Whipping an apron around her waist, she said, "You three go without me. I promised Halah I'd show her how to make the world's best brownies."

No one rivals Cleo's brownies.

"Brownies? Awesome." Halah clearly missed Cleo's memo.

Inga danced at my feet, leash in her mouth.

"What about Beau?" I asked. He was asleep on the couch with the rubber Kong.

Cleo shrugged. "Beau's out for the count. Digging up your flower beds wore him out."

I found an old iPod and gave it to Cristina to use. I snagged my Samsung Galaxy, set up a playlist, and stuffed the leash in my pocket.

"Stay close, Inga," I said, and she led the way.

It was a quiet night and traffic was light. It felt good to pound the pavement with my sneakers. We started off at a slow jog, down the alley and headed for the school track.

Deep in our own thoughts, we missed the long, stretched car that creeped up behind us. The lights were snuffed and the engine, if it purred, jammed with the music in my ear. We were blindsided. Two men captured us from the rear, pinning our arms and dragging us to the curb. I fought my attacker but he was two hundred fifty pounds of cement. The driver pulled the limo to the curb and opened the back door. I screamed for Inga. She jumped in the backseat and plopped onto Kyle Tierney's lap.

Kyle, the traitor beagle, and the guy with the big gun stuffed in his belt sat on one seat. Cristina and I took the other. Cement guy rode shotgun.

I was too flippin' mad to speak. I wrestled my pockets for a taser or an AK-47. I found a leash to choke them with, Dr. Pepper Lip Smacker, and a gold cigarette lighter. I set the recorder, smeared my lips, and dropped the lighter and Smacker on the seat beside me.

"Kyle." Cristina almost choked on the word.

Tierney pressed a button and spoke to the driver. "You guys got a sandwich up there?"

The driver lowered the partition and tossed back a Ken-Tones bag. Tierney fed the hamburger to Inga.

"Your beagle likes me."

"She likes anybody with food. She's a well known food whore," I said.

Cristina crossed a leg and smoothed her hair. "I just got back," she said all sultry. "I was going to call you."

"*Seriously?* You're going with that line?" I said.

Tierney blew a deep sigh. "I was good to you. Why'd you play me like that?"

Cristina did that blink blink and a pouty thing with her mouth. "I know I was stupid, Kyle. I wish I could take it all back."

"You gonna take back four years in a box?" His voice tightened. "I've been countin' the days to return the favor."

"Whoa," I said. "You don't have a shovel in the trunk, do you?"

He shrugged. "She owes me. I'm here to collect."

Cristina wrung my arm in a death grip. "Do something."

"To be fair," I said reasonably, "Cristina didn't pull the trigger."

"She's as responsible for Mitchell's death as I am."

"How does that work?"

He glanced sideways at Cristina. Her cheeks colored, and she looked at her hands. "We had a business deal. But Cristina wanted it all. The switch was her idea."

Cristina opened her mouth to deny it and changed her mind.

"You're talking about Marilyn's earrings," I said, wanting to be clear for the gold lighter.

Tierney sighed with what appeared to be genuine regret. "The kid was scared. His hand shook, and I caught the switch. We struggled. The gun went off."

"If it was an accident, why not tell the cops?"

"Cristina saw what happened. If she made a statement, the charge would've been reduced."

"Why didn't you?" I said jabbing her in ribs.

"Owww."

"Cuz she didn't give a shit. She took the money and earrings and ran."

"Back-up," I said. "What money?"

"I advanced her ten grand against her share of the sale. And then there was the ten grand for the ticket."

That's another juicy tidbit she neglected to mention.

Cristina sniffed. "You try driving to California. It takes a lot of gas."

"I prefer the cash. And the earrings," Tierney said. "I'll collect one way or another."

I said, "I get it. Cristina screwed you over. You wanted to get back at her. Is that why you killed Billy?"

"This again?"

"Billy was looking for your safe. He wanted to rip you off."

Kyle fed Inga more sandwich. "Lots of people try to rip me off. It's life. I deal with it."

Cristina said, "I didn't take your stupid earrings. I saw you wrestle them away from Alan."

His voice was chipped ice. "Liar."

"I think Cristina's telling the truth." *For once,* I thought to myself. "She came back to Chicago to steal them one more time."

Tierney growled. "Diamonds don't disappear into thin air."

Cristina's voice sounded small. "I need more time to come up with the money."

"You had four years, babe. Your clock just ran out."

"Whoa," I said. "My clock's still ticking."

I chewed my lip and wracked my brain. *Where were the bloody earrings?*

I had to believe they were both telling the truth. Neither snagged the earrings that night. It's like they disappeared in thin air.

And then the crime scene photograph flashed in my head. The blood. The body on the floor. The discarded earrings. Like scattered pieces to a puzzle. The answer came to me then in one sweet moment, devoid of hoopla.

A giggle welled in my throat, and I swallowed it. A goofy grin spread over my face. It wasn't an attractive say-cheese smile. It was a Donny Osmond beamer.

"Before you go all bad-ass, I think we can work something out," I said.

"You're oddly cheery," Kyle said. "Keep talking."

"You don't have the earrings." I cut my thumb in Cristina's direction. "She doesn't have the earrings."

"She's a damn liar."

"Granted. But this time she's telling the truth."

My cheesy grin got bigger.

"Why are you doing that with your mouth," Cristina said.

"I know where Marilyn's earrings are."

"You're bluffing," Tierney said.

"I'm a hotshot detective," I snapped. "And a damn good one."

"Okay. Where are they?"

I tried to lose the grin, but it was a stickler. "If I told you that, you wouldn't need me now, would you?"

"Okay. But Cristina stays with me. She's my insurance policy."

"Cristina's a pain in the ass," I admitted. "And as tempting as your offer sounds, she comes with me. She's got a kid. Halah doesn't deserve to lose her mama just because she's a dumb ass."

Cristina blink blinked. "That was sweet."

"The earrings," Kyle said. "When will you have them?"

"Gimme a week."

"You got forty-eight hours. Then I'm coming for the both of you."

"You don't scare me," I lied.

I jerked the door open. Cristina shoved me aside, trampled over me, and dived out the door.

I lugged the beagle off Tierney's lap, and he followed me out the door. Inga tooted. It smelled like rotten sausages.

"You're embarrassing," I told her.

"You think the dog's embarrassing?"

I followed his gaze to Cristina, butt-tuckin' it full speed down the street.

"What?" I asked.

He shook his head. "I used to date her."

The Tierney encounter took the good bye out of Cristina's farewell party.

I choked the words out. "You'll have to stay a few days until we get this thing sorted out."

The three high-fived and Halah passed around her brownies.

I wrote out a list and handed Cleo the paper. "Would you put these together for me?"

Cleo read the list out loud. "Four shovels. Oreos. Sandwiches. Flashlights. Large thermos of hot coffee. Flowers. What is this?"

"Our supplies to get Marilyn's diamond earrings."

Cristina gasped. "I thought you were bluffing. Where are they?"

"You'll know when we get there."

"You don't trust me."

"Not even a little bit."

"When do we get the diamonds?" Cristina asked.

"Tomorrow is Billy's funeral. We'll go the next night."

"Awesome!" Halah said.

I shook my head. "Not you, chica. You and Inga will stay with Mama. You're both too young to go to county jail and tango with a big woman named Bertha."

Cristina laughed. "She's joking. Right?"

Cleo shrugged. "The cops arrested me last summer on some bullshit charge."

"Wow," Halah said.

I said, "Cleo learned a valuable lesson. You can't threaten to kill people."

My assistant winked. "I really learned to tango faster than big Bertha."

Chapter Twenty-three

I shut the lights off behind my parting guests and went to bed. A sound woke me in the night. I lay still, listening. There it was again. The scruff of a footstep outside my window.

My breath caught in my chest. I poked Inga beside me. "Did you hear that?"

The beagle snored softly.

My eyes shot to the dark shadow of a man outside my window. He jarred the frame, trying to force it open. I shook Inga with both hands.

"Kill!"

She opened an eye and stretched.

"No more sausages."

I rolled off the bed, snagged the phone with one hand, and stuffed the other in a dresser drawer. The 9mm trembled in my grip. I shook a bra off the barrel and punched a number on my cell. Mama has Father Timothy on speed dial. I have Rocco.

My brother picked up. I didn't wait for him to speak.

"Someone's breaking in."

Rocco's running footsteps pounded the floor.

"Stay with me, Cat." A door slammed and Rocco was on his way. I was glad my brother wears pajamas.

Rocco's breath was jagged. He was running to the car.

"If the asshole makes it in before I get there—"

Glass shattered and my premium platinum alarm system screamed. Inga howled.

"Shoot him!" Rocco yelled.

I threw down the phone and released the safety on my Glock. The alarm lit up every room in the house and flooded the exterior with light. The prowler would almost certainly flee. I high-tailed to the front window and jerked back the curtain. The skinny guy was in the spotlight, hightailing it to the dark street. He would've made it. But just before he cleared the lawn and hit the dark street, his right foot caught on an in-ground sprinkler. His arms flapped wildly, but they couldn't restore his balance or give him flight. The bungler toppled flat on his face, one leg hideously tangled. He looked over his shoulder and our eyes locked. His face, racked with pain, was caught in the floodlights.

Devin stumbled to his feet and, with one leg dragging, hobbled into the night.

I turned off the alarm and Inga stopped howling. Rocco screeched to the curb. He raced up the steps all bad ass in his PJ's and slippers. They were the Batman ones his daughters bought him last year for Christmas.

Rocco charged inside.

"He got away," I said.

My brother put an arm around me, and the dreaded adrenalin crashed. I started shaking and couldn't stop. Rocco pried the pistol from my hand before I shot up the room.

Rocco poured me a brandy, and I sat on the couch wrapped in a comforter. He searched the room, inside and out, and nailed a chunk of plywood over the broken window.

My brother found a box of Tino's pizza in the fridge. He brought out paper plates, a jar of garlic-stuffed green olives, hot peppers, and a couple beers to wash everything down.

"I talked to your neighbor," he said. "The one who wears binoculars around her neck."

"Mrs. Pickins. The neighborhood snoop."

"She gave me a good description of the perp. She didn't recognize him."

Spy-eyes doesn't drive. She'd have no reason to hang out at Jack's Auto Shop.

"Apparently the guy took a head-dive running away," Rocco said. "Mrs. Pickins said he has a gash on his head and a bum leg."

"Karma's a bitch."

He eyed me curiously. "She said you got a good look at him."

"He was scrawny. Wore a lot of black."

"And you have no idea who he was?"

I shrugged.

Here's the thing. Devin is an idiot. Last spring he stole some Australian red and pink diamonds from me. I stole them back. Now he thinks the diamonds are his and that I have them.

Well, they aren't and I don't.

I thought maybe if I could convince Devin the diamonds are gone, he would go away. I wanted to handle this with minimal bloodshed. Devin was pissing me off, but I didn't need the DeLuca men to kill him. At least not yet.

I said, "Thanks. Is that your Batmobile parked in front?"

"It is, Robin."

"Maria will be worried."

"She was worried about you." He dragged another slice from the box. "I called her. She's okay now."

I tucked the comforter around me. "I'm okay too. You can go home now, bro."

"Not a chance."

Rocco sat beside me on the couch. I slept the rest of the night with my head on his shoulder.

Chapter Twenty-four

Billy was to be buried at one-thirty. I had one last chance to find his St. Christopher necklace.

I parked across the street from the strip poker house as the two women drove off in a late model Mazda sedan. I gripped my first cup of coffee like a lifeline and nibbled on a bagel. The ogre opened the door and grabbed the paper off the porch. Damn. The big oaf looked like a slow reader.

I opened up my Laura Caldwell novel and kept an eye on the front door. Billy's funeral was at eleven-thirty. If the big guy wasn't out of the house by nine, I would text two words to Cleo. *Plan D.*

Last night I told Cleo I was going after Billy's St. Christopher. I said, "If the roomies don't leave, we're onto Plan B."

"What's Plan B?"

"Plan B is where you kiss your Camry good bye. You drive by and smash into one of their cars. My crazy cousin Frankie arrives on the scene with sirens blaring. The roomies come out. I sneak in and find Billy's St. Christopher before the funeral."

"I gotta go with C or D.

"What's C?"

Plan C is me smashing their car with the Silver Bullet."

"Watch your mouth."

"Or Plan D. You make me a partner."

"I have a partner."

"So have Inga burst their car into flames."

"You do flames?"

"I'll torch the sucker."

I thought about it. "An explosion would buy me extra time."

"Everyone loves fireworks." She grinned. "Partner?"

I winced. "Torch away. But only if I text *Plan D*."

"Yahoo!"

"And you have to promise not to shoot anybody."

Cleo didn't like it. She blew her lips. "Fine. But I do not speak for Frankie."

At 8:55 I ditched the book and stared bleakly at my phone. I was running out of time. I closed my eyes and evoked the saints. There had to be thousands of them. I figured one of them could boot that guy out the door.

When I opened my eyes, the ogre was strolling to his car. He wore jeans and sneakers. Maybe he worked construction.

I rolled my eyes up and winked at the saints.

I texted Cleo. *No fireworks.*

When he was gone, I skipped up the steps and let myself in.

The living room was a wash of warm yellows and browns. The furnishings were surprisingly chic for this blue-collar neighborhood. A painting above the hearth was a Julian Ritter original. Maybe it fell off the back of a truck like Uncle Joey's scotch.

Frankly, I didn't care. I was here for one thing. Billy's funeral was in a few hours. And if St. Christopher cared at all about his necklace, he'd give me a shout-out. I listened. Chris was the strong, silent type.

I made my way through the dining room, kitchen, and master bedroom with the Jacuzzi bath. The master rooms smelled of musk. The clothes in the walk-in closet were ogre-sized. The master bath had a supply of unused toothbrushes and women's toiletries—presumably for guests. Even ogres get lucky.

When I had exhausted the downstairs possibilities, I moved up the staircase along a curved banister and down a carpeted hall. The house had two bedrooms upstairs, an exercise room, and a bathroom at the end of the hall. I guessed the bedrooms belonged to the woman who beat Billy at strip poker. One room was showcase neat. The other was a scream for my Merry Maid.

I searched quickly and methodically. Rummaging through drawers, sliding open closet doors, and peering under beds. I was running out of rooms and losing hope fast.

The jewelry box was in the messy room on the unmade bed. It was buried in a small mountain of clothes. Not intentionally. She seemed to have tried on a dozen outfits before deciding what to wear today. I wondered where she went.

It was a music box from Tiffany's. When I opened it, a dancing ballerina spun around to "Edelweiss." A keepsake, perhaps, from childhood.

Under the ballerina was Billy's St Christopher's necklace. The necklace I had seen hundreds of times had transformed since confirmation day. The surface was worn almost smooth from Billy's constant fingering of his good luck charm. The personal inscription had long disappeared.

I draped the necklace around my neck and gave St. Christopher a thumbs-up. Tucking the jewelry box under the mountain of clothes, I made one sweeping glance around the room before hustling down the hallway.

Halfway down the steps the doorknob turned. *Crap.* Maybe the ogre wasn't a construction worker after all. Maybe he went to the store for milk and smokes.

I scrambled back up the steps and made a nose-dive under the messy woman's bed. I didn't expect her to vacuum the floor anytime soon.

The dust tickled my nostrils. I squeezed the bridge of my nose to stifle a sneeze. He came in talking on his cell.

"Next weekend works for m—She's not coming. Cuz it's over, Ma….No, you can't call her. It doesn't matter why we broke up… Okay. She's a slut. I'm done with her.…Tell you what. I'll come down next weekend, take you both out to dinner.…I know it's Pa's birthday (laughs). Don't ask me what I got him.…He weasels it out of you.…A hint, then. It's for his train collection. That's all

I'll say….He's never seen anything like it….Don't worry about the money, Ma. I got a big promotion at work….Love you, too.

Ogres have nosey mothers too.

I decided he was alone. He rattled dishes in the kitchen. Probably getting something to eat.

After a while, he turned on the television in the living room. He was settling in. I was trapped.

I had already checked every room for an exit strategy. In the business of stalking people, things can get sticky. A balcony or big tree to throw myself in may come in handy. There was a sorry lack of ledges and fire-escapes in the ogre's house. And I didn't bring a parachute.

I texted Max with the ogre's address and a brief note. *Hiding upstairs. Distract ogre. Will exit kitchen. Alley.*

Max texted back. *Fee. Fi. Fo. Fum.*

Twelve agonizing minutes later, the doorbell rang.

I zoomed to the head of the stairs and held my breath. The TV muted. The door opened.

Max's voice boomed. "Good morning, sir. I represent Chi-Town Polling. We're asking people in Bridgeport about their favorite Chicago style pizza."

"Not interested."

"I'll only take a moment of your time."

"Go away."

"Italian sausage and mushroom? Or pepperoni and olive?"

The ogre growled. "Your foot is in my door."

"Anchovies?"

I slipped out the kitchen door and flew down the alley. The Hummer trolled down the side street and parked to intercept me. Max got out.

He took my hands and looked me over.

"Are you okay, Kitten?"

"I'm fine. Thanks for the lift."

"I would have gone with you."

I smiled. "Who would pick us up? We can't all fit in Cleo's Corvette."

Some Like It Hot   137

"We do if you sit on my lap. What did you learn?"

"The ogre's girlfriend dumped him. He bought his dad something for his train collection." I sneezed. "And it's a dust fest under that bed."

"That's it?"

I waggled the St. Christopher from around my neck and beamed. "It was in a jewelry box."

"You rock."

My pocket vibrated. I grappled behind me and dragged out my cell phone.

"Pants on Fire Detective Agency."

Uncle Joey lowered his voice to a whisper. "Where are you? This gig starts in half an hour."

I squawked. "Omigod! Billy's funeral."

Max shoved me in the Hummer. He flew across town zigzagging in and out of traffic, climbing the sidewalks twice to avoid slowing down.

He braked hard at my door.

I ran inside and raced to the bathroom. I brushed my teeth, swirled mouthwash while splashing perfume and slapping blush on my cheeks and Dr. Peppering my lips. I finger combed my hair back in a honey bun and squirmed into pantyhose and a black Jackie-Kennedy style A-line dress and Ferragamo pumps. I grabbed a soft plum silk scarf, my black Fendi bag, and flew out the door in four minutes, thirty nine seconds. A personal record.

Max drove like a madman. If I wasn't rolling in a tank, I would have made my peace with God.

"Do you want me to come in with you?"

I checked Max out. Always a pleasure. He was dressed in a white tee with four floating heads of the Grateful Dead and a pair of black Levi's. Maybe not the best choice for a funeral.

"Billy loved the Grateful Dead," I admitted. "And Ben & Jerry's Cherry Garcia was his favorite ice cream."

"I have a sports coat in the back. It'll cover most of the heads."

"Why not? It'll make Billy smile."

The street in front of the church was lined with parked cars. Max jetted to the curb and parked by the fire hydrant.

"You'll just make it. Knock 'em dead."

Max grabbed his jacket and we hit the ground running.

I said, "Stall Father Timothy. I need a minute."

The church was packed. Bridgeport is a tight-knit community. We show up for funerals and any other community event that involves food.

Billy's family jammed the first few rows. People reconnect at funerals. There were waves and whispers in the pews. I saw friends I hadn't seen since high school.

My twin brothers were there. They're big guys and easy to spot in a crowd. Michael and Vinnie were younger than Billy and didn't really know him. But they knew Mama was cooking.

Cleo sat on an aisle seat honking into a hankie. It's tough to lose someone you knew seven whole hours.

Captain Bob stood in the back of the church next to Papa. They ran Billy out of town. I hadn't seen Billy again until the other day.

Captain Bob's daughter stomped past her father and kicked his shin. I glared at Papa and made a mental note to smack him later.

I dipped my fingers in holy water and crossed myself. Billy was laid out in front of the altar, positioned under a light. The beam gave him a halo-like glow. Billy would laugh his socks off.

The golden bronze casket was a top of the line "Sleeping With Angels" model. Grandpa bought one last year when he had pneumonia. He got stuck with it when he didn't kick the bucket. He took out the extra cot in the guest room and placed it beside the double bed.

I marched to the front of the sanctuary. I could see Max blocking Father Timothy in the wing. I quickened my pace and decided he only appeared to have the priest in a choke hold.

I stood at the casket with my back to the crowd. I removed the St. Christopher necklace from around my neck, gently lifted Billy's head, and slipped it around him.

Then I touched his face and said good bye. His skin felt cold and empty. I didn't know where Billy went, but he sure as hell wasn't in there.

When I turned around again, Mrs. Bonham's sad eyes smiled.

Chapter Twenty-five

I brought a tropical fruit salad and bottle of wine to the wake. I threw in some boxes of Ding Dongs for Billy.

Mama organized the food while I helped the ladies in the kitchen until Mama kicked me out.

She stuffed a cookie in my hand and whispered, "The gossip stops when the kids are around."

I had to wonder if she remembered I'm thirty.

I directed traffic to the backyard where Papa and Uncle Rudy set up chairs borrowed from the church. Father Timothy made the rounds, praying with people and making them cry. I figured Billy wouldn't want people to be sad at his party. I ducked every time I saw the priest coming.

I knew most of the people there. But I kept an eye open for a woman with Kansas written all over her. I didn't know if Nicole Bonham would show. Or even what she looked like. Mrs. Bonham wasn't exactly displaying pictures of the evil daughter-in-law.

Uncle Joey and Linda two-stepped around, topping wine glasses and passing out Ding Dongs. Aunt Fran was in charge of keeping Grandma DeLuca from wandering off and joining the circus. Nonni had been thinking a lot about gypsies lately. When she was a child, gypsy trapeze artists came to her Italian village. There were fortune tellers and clowns. Gypsy children sold candied walnuts and sticky pistachio buns. It sounded more fun than living with Aunt Izzie.

Aunt Francesca and Nonni sat with Mrs. Bonham. Friends paraded by with hugs and kind words about Billy. Aunt Fran held Mrs. Bonham's hand and slipped her fresh tissues. She didn't see Grandma DeLuca pinch drinks from the guests' hands.

"I hoped Billy would marry Caterina," Mrs. Bonham confided in a voice half the room heard.

"If only he had," Aunt Fran bemoaned.

"Your niece has a nice young man now."

Francesca sniffed. "You clearly don't know who he works for."

"Musholini," Grandma DeLuca slurred.

"The FBI turned down my son Frankie. He was too good for them."

Mrs. Bonham's spine stiffened. "Cat is a daughter to me. She's not responsible for Frankie's screw-ups."

You go, girl.

"Caterina insults my boy," Aunt Fran hissed. "She spits on my face."

Papa crossed the room. He gave his mama a cup of coffee and took the empty whiskey glass from her hand.

Rocco tilted his head. "Is Papa stepping on Fran's foot?"

I nodded. "Grinding away."

Aunt Fran gasped.

Papa said, "Don't disrespect my daughter. Or the father of my future grandchildren."

A flurry of whispers surfed the room. *Caterina's getting married? Who wudda thought?*

I spun around and my forever friend, Melanie, wagged a finger.

"We're supposed to be best friends, Cat. Your switched-at-birth sister just told me you're pregnant with Max's child."

Rocco choked and ducked for cover.

My sister hates me. "Kill me now," I said.

"Sophie heard it from Grant. How the hell does he get to know? I'm your best friend. Grant hasn't been around since high school."

I cradled my throbbing head.

She sniffed, all injured. "Does Savino know?"

I looked behind me and caught my breath. "Where did she go?"

"I know what you're doing. You're not changing the subject."

I grabbed Melanie's arm. "A woman just came in. Did you see her? Black dress, big sunglasses.

"It's a Prada. I would kill for that dress."

I shook her. "Where did she go?"

"Your diversion tactics aren't working. Are you, or are you not naming the baby after me?"

"Arrghh!"

I made a quick search of the dining room, kitchen, and backyard. No one remembered seeing her.

Prada dress? Gucci sunglasses? Not exactly how I pictured Billy's wife. Well, love makes us crazy. And then I remembered the things Billy and Mrs. Bonham said about Nicole. The word wasn't crazy. It was greedy.

I nudged through the crowd and down the hallway to Billy's bedroom. I pushed through the door.

The woman in black was trying to open Billy's window. It was stuck. There was a large manila envelope in her hand.

"An odd exit strategy," I said.

"It's stuffy in here. I was getting air."

"Give me what you have there."

"It's mine. It's a picture of my cousin and me."

Not the crazy wife after all.

"If that's true, Mrs. Bonham will give it to you after the party. She'll even let you go out the door."

"Mind your own business."

"Billy *is* my business. And my partner."

Her eyes flickered something I couldn't read.

I said, "Are you the cousin Billy went to camp with that summer?"

"That's me."

"That's funny. Cuz Billy didn't have a cousin. And he never went to camp."

"I'm taking my picture. You can't stop me."

I looked her over. She was about my height. Twenty-five pounds heavier. But she didn't have my three brothers.

I would have her for lunch.

"There are a dozen cops down the hall who are really pissed their friend was killed. What do you think they'll do to the thief at his wake?"

She threw the envelope on the floor and pushed past me out the door.

I hunkered down on Billy's bed and opened the envelope. They weren't childhood pictures. Or even family pictures. They were surveillance photos. Billy playing Bogie. Two men in the park. One little white dog.

The big man looked like he could live at the top of a beanstalk. It was the guy from the strip poker house.

The other guy would be Billy's client's husband. I caught the file in Billy's office. They were involved in a bitter custody battle over Coochie, the Bichon Frisé in the photo. Billy was stalking the husband and Coochie when he took the photographs in the envelope. The wife hired him to steal her dog back.

I stuffed the picture back in the envelope and raced after her. I tore down the front steps and out into the street.

The Prada woman in black had disappeared.

I went back to the wake but left early. It wasn't much fun once people started stripping drinks from the pregnant woman's hand.

I buzzed by Billy's office for the little white dog's file. Half an hour later, I was in Coochie's living room with a martini in my hand.

Jamie Peterson was slim with lots of curly auburn hair tipped blond. Her nails were painted sapphire blue with little fake diamonds glued on. I thought they were cool. The piercings under a brow were a matter of personal taste.

"I saw you at the funeral," Jamie said. "Someone said you were engaged to Billy."

That would be Cleo. "It was a really long time ago."

"I didn't go to the wake. I don't know Billy's mom or anybody there. So I came home, and made my own drink to say good bye to Bill."

I didn't tell her how hard it was for me to get a drink at that wake.

I lifted my glass. "To Billy. One of the good guys."

"Good bye, Billy."

Her drink spilled a little. She'd been saying a lot of good byes since the funeral.

"He loved my martinis."

"I'm sure he did." Billy was an equal opportunity drinker.

Jamie slammed her drink and popped a fat olive in her mouth. I suspected a half dozen of those would be dinner.

"How long were you and Billy partners?"

"Not long."

I thought that sounded better than *ten hours.*

I said, "I've begun going through Billy's files. He left a few open cases. I'd like to finish them for him."

"You should get drunk first."

She took the martini pitcher from the table and filled our glasses. This time we got two fat olives.

I flashed the photo I snagged from the woman in black. "Billy took this picture in the park."

She squinted. "That's my husband and Coochie. The guy could just be someone Will met at the park. Will's a salesman. Never met a guy he didn't try to sell a car to."

A light clicked on in my head. Peterson Ford. "Last year my brothers bought twin cars from your husband."

She sniffed. "Bill was going to get Coochie back for me. She doesn't like Will very much. She wouldn't come when he called her."

"So how did he get her?"

"Will's an asshole. I kicked him out last month. And I gave him a list of the things I want in the divorce. He said, 'Okay. I want Coochie.' I said, 'Over my dead body.' So he comes back the next day and calls her. I call her too. For the first time *ever,*

Coochie runs to him. He scoops her up. He runs out the door and big slices of bacon fall out of his pants."

"Weasel," I said.

Jamie slugged down her drink. "Coochie is all I have left. The things on the list I gave Will? *Stolen*. Every last thing on my list. The cops aren't saying. But I think it was the Bridgeport Bandit."

"That's an extraordinary coincidence."

My money was on the weasel husband. I've seen my share of nasty break-ups and disgruntled partners who'd cut off their own nose before giving up a tissue. I once had a client whose husband drove a bulldozer through their house so she wouldn't get it in the divorce.

I reached in my bag and pulled out a card. "Billy and I were partners. Call me next week. I'll get Coochie back for you."

"I'll pay whatever you say. But I gotta tell you, Will is nobody's fool. He's scary. He won't give up Coochie without a fight. He's into that martial arts crap."

"I've got a scarier Special Forces guy. He can kill with his bare hands."

Jamie smiled through an alcohol-induced haze. "For that I will pay extra."

I swung home and picked up my partner. She rode shotgun, head out the window, ears flapping in the wind. She was on the hunt for a guy who stuffs bacon in his pants.

Peterson Ford is about fifteen minutes north of Bridgeport on Dayton. I'd never met Will Peterson but, like many Chi-Towners, I could pick him out in a crowd. Peterson advertises his cars on late night TV. He wears a plaid sports coat and loud ties. But what sets him apart from all other late night car salesmen is his nose. It's a colossal honker.

I pulled into the car lot and two salesmen fought each other to get to me first. I wrestled them off and browsed around on my own.

The building was lots of glass and steel. Inga and I walked outside long enough to find Will Peterson's office through the window. He was alone at his desk. Jamie's little white Bichon Frisé was curled up in a dog bed by the door. I nudged my partner. Then we walked inside.

"Bacon," I whispered and dropped Inga's leash.

She was off to the races.

I skipped into the office. "Mr. Peterson, I'm so sorry." I gushed and stopped. "Inga?"

The beagle was sitting on his lap. Staring at his nose like it was a sausage. I forced my own eyes away. He was freakin' Pinocchio.

"She likes me."

He let her down, and the dogs did their butt sniffing ritual. He smoothed his plaid coat and shook my hand.

"Call me Will."

"Cat DeLuca. You have a beautiful girl. What's her name?"

"Coochie. She's good company. What do you call your beagle?"

"Her name is Inga. I haven't had her long," I lied. "She belonged to my ex."

"Really? Coochie was my wife's dog. We're still getting to know each other."

"Us too."

He winked. "Let me guess. You took the dog cuz your ex took your car. And you're here looking for a new one."

I willed my eyes away from his nose. "How did you know? Oh. Is that what happened to you too? You had to take the dog cuz she took everything else?"

He tapped his head and winked. "Not if you're smart. There are ways to almost have it all."

I took his arm in a chummy gesture. "Do tell."

He laughed and his hand covered mine. "Come along, kids. I want to show Cat some cars."

I punched Savino's number on my phone and heard voices in the background. He was at FBI headquarters, hard at work catching bad guys.

"How was the funeral, babe?" Chance asked. "I wish I could've been there."

"I am glad it's over. I caught up with some old friends. It was like a mini high school reunion."

"Sounds like Billy would've liked it."

"Yeah, you're right. So, you hungry?"

"I'm starving. I was just thinking about ordering a sandwich. It's not looking like I'm not getting out of here anytime soon."

Dammit. "Oh well."

"There's that new Ethiopian restaurant not far from the office. I could escape the office for a quick dinner with the most beautiful woman in Bridgeport."

"Well, I don't know about her, but I have a thing."

"What kind of a thing?"

"It's just a thing."

"Does this have anything to do with the break-in Rocco told me about?"

Rocco has such a big mouth! "My brother embellishes."

"When were you going to tell me about it, DeLucky?"

"At the thing," I lied. "It's at the Moose Lodge."

"Is your mama cooking?"

"You know she is."

"I'm on my way."

I was waiting outside the Moose Lodge when Chance drove up in his Toyota Highlander Hybrid. Somebody had hung a huge banner over the doorway. DEVIN'S SOBRIETY PARTY. YAY!

Savino kissed me. "You didn't tell me Devin was home."

"Didn't I?"

"What's it been?" He counted his fingers. "Five months sober?"

I looked at my watch. "More like five minutes."

He watched my eyes. "Has he bothered you?"

"Nothing I can't handle."

I put my arms around his waist. "Do you see the white Lincoln parked across the street. Greasy guy behind the wheel?"

"Hmmm. Who is he?"

That's Freddy the Fence. He owns a pawn shop on West Cermark Road. Devin stiffed him on some merchandise he had promised him last spring. So now his latest hobby is stalking Devin. It's scaring the shit out of him."

"Let me make sure I have this right. He's leaning on Devin for the Australian diamonds. And Devin thinks you still have them?"

"It's a vicious circle, isn't it?"

Savino crossed the street to the white Lincoln. The driver saw him coming and slid down in his seat. Chance tapped on the window and flashed his badge. I tiptoed across the street and ducked behind the guy's bumper. I was all ears.

"Sir, step out of the car please."

Freddy the Fence was a short box-shaped man with lego-shaped hair and weasel-shaped facial features. He wore an expensive suit to impress, but instead mimicked too many bad gangster movies.

"The FBI wants to know what your interest is in Devin Rivera."

"Who?"

"Mr. Rivera is currently under surveillance. We're monitoring his activities and his associates."

"The name doesn't ring a bell."

"I checked you out, Freddy. Captain Maxfield from the Ninth Precinct tells me you're being investigated for trafficking stolen goods."

Freddy the Fence's throat sounded parched. "I run a legitimate business."

"Of course you do."

"Hey. You have me confused with somebody else."

"Rivera claims he has merchandise he, in fact, does not have. Last week, a shooting over this fantasy merchandise resulted in the death of an undercover agent."

"That sucks."

"Be assured, Devin Rivera is going down, Freddy. You do not want to have any connection with him that we will trace. Is that understood?"

"There's no connection." He sputtered a nervous laugh. "My car died. That's why I stopped here."

"We're watching you." Savino handed him a card. "Start it."

"Excuse me?"

"Start the car."

Freddy the Fence crammed his squatty frame behind the wheel and reluctantly turned the key. The engine purred.

His brow lifted. "Go figure."

"It's a bloody miracle," Savino said.

As I watched Freddy the Fence burn rubber, I got up and glanced across the street. Devin pulled back from the window. He was watching the whole time. Damn.

I wrapped my arms around Chance's neck and kissed his lips. "You know, you're totally gorgeoulicious when you're bad ass."

Savino laughed a deep throaty laugh in my ear, hooked his arm around my waist, and we joined the party.

There was a good turn out. A lot of people sipped iced tea and thought of getting a beer on the way home. Pink Floyd pumped through clumsy, outdated speakers. A large table was lined up with soft drinks and all things non-alcoholic. There were pizzas from Tino's Deli and Mama made meatballs and pasta and antipasto. At the center of the table, a chocolate fudge cake from Bridgeport Bakery on Archer Avenue said WE'RE PROUD OF YOU, DEVIN. It was decorated with lots of gooey frosting and tiny models of really cool cars. Like the ones Devin likes to cut up in his chop shop.

Across the room, Mama held Devin's face in her hands. She said something that made him smile. I suspected she told us the same things when we got in trouble. Then she patted his cheek and stuffed a heaping plate of food in his hands.

Papa walked over and slapped Devin on the back. I think he knocked the air out of him. Devin looked like he wanted to bolt.

The last time Papa saw Devin was the night Devin assaulted me. Papa crushed his fingers and stood on his face. The next day Devin went into treatment.

"What's your dad saying?" Savino asked.

"He's rubbing his scar," I said. "He is saying, 'We all have our battles. I'm proud of ya, son. But touch my daughter again, and I will whack ya.'" And then Papa smacked him again.

Devin's eyes darted around the room. They rested on the studalicious guy beside me who could dismember him without working up a sweat. His eyes flashed terror.

"I think he got the message," Chance said.

"I'm not sure. He's a special kind of stupid."

Chance kissed my cheek and began working his way across the room. Halfway there, my switched-at-birth sister Sophie grabbed his hand and dragged him away. I hung out at the buffet table and filled two paper plates with fettuccine carbonara, mediterranean green salad, and big crusty rolls.

I paused at the dessert table, eenie-meenie-miny mo-ing my pointy finger between the pignoli pie and the tiramisu.

Papa chortled behind me. "Take one of each. It's what I do."

"Smart," I agreed and did so.

Papa glanced furtively around the room saying, "Your Mama can't hear, can she?"

She was twenty feet away consoling one of Sophie's screaming toddlers. I couldn't be sure. Mama has freakish ears.

"Whisper," I said.

He glanced at Mama's back, and she turned and waved.

I laughed. "And I thought you were faithful cuz you're a good man."

He grinned. "Your Mama sees to it."

My parents adore each other. They met when Mama was a hat-check girl at the Berghoff downtown. One night a guy bowled past her and snagged Walter Payton's leather coat. Papa was the rookie cop who responded to the call. When he got there, the thief was on the floor, all tied up in knots with Payton's leather belt. The way Papa tells it, the hat-check girl had the most beautiful legs he'd ever seen. She was a curvy five-foot five, a hundred fifteen pounds. The thief was six feet tall and built like a refrigerator. The guy didn't stand a chance.

Neither did Papa. He and Mama were married four months later.

"What's up?" I said.

He winced. "I need your help. Our thirty-fifth anniversary is coming up. Your Mama wants to get married."

"You're not married? Jeez, Papa. Does Grandma DeLuca know?"

He made a face. "Some church busy-body told your Mama, if you're married by a judge, then God doesn't know you're married.

"God's not a fool. You have five kids. He can figure it out."

Papa grabbed his scar. "Your Mama wants a church ceremony. With Father Timothy. She says we have to write our own vows."

"What did you say?"

"I said, *Yes, dear*. I'm not a fool either."

I laughed. "Okay. I'll talk to her. Maybe I can help with the reception. We'll make it fun."

"Fun? I doubt I can drink that much alcohol. But I intend to try." He lowered his voice to a whisper. "I want you to write my vows. I don't know what to say."

"I'll get the cake and the booze. I'm not writing your vows."

"Of course you are." He kissed my cheek. "And get on it. I gotta memorize this shit."

Chance shook off Sophie and closed in on Devin. Devin saw him coming and tried to make his escape, but Chance caught his hand and squeezed. Savino seemed to empty the blood from Devin's hand. It went to his cheeks. His face, racked with pain, bulged a hideous red. I almost felt sorry for him.

Chance leaned in and whispered something in his ear. He released him and Devin ran to the bathroom, hand over mouth. He was going to be sick.

Mama did a little trapping of her own. She and Father Timothy had captured Savino. Now it was him I felt sorry for. Not sorry enough to save his ass, but it was close.

Father Timothy was deep in conversation about reserving the church. Mama eyes were in nonstop scan mode across the room, anxious for me to join the conversion. But I've known since I was five that my mama never looks under the table.

When Chance found me again, he growled in my ear. "You know, you could have saved me from your mother."

"Who?" I gulped my fruit punch. "I have no idea what you're talking about. By the way, whatcha say to Devin?"

He shrugged. "Guy talk."

Jack strolled over beaming. "Great party, kids. Thanks for coming." He turned to Chance. "I saw you over there with Devin. Whatever you said, hit home. He got all choked up."

"It was a powerful moment, Jack," I said. "I think they bonded."

Jack looked a little choked himself. "Thank you."

The cobalt blues smiled. "I wouldn't have missed it for the world."

Chapter Twenty-six

I woke in a sweat, chased by a giant, gold-toothed ogre in my dreams. I listened. The only sound was Inga's snore.

The grandfather clock in the living room chimed four times. I groaned and pulled the covers over my head.

Then I sat up straight in bed. I replayed the conversation in my head.

I'm here for my friend, I said. I only care about his St. Christopher necklace.

We don't know the guy.

Blah blah blah. I fast forwarded the conversation in my head.

Tell you what, the gold toothed ogre said. Buy his mother another St. Christopher necklace. She won't know the difference.

I shook my partner. The snoring stopped. Inga pretended to sleep.

"I know you can hear me," I said.

I plopped down on my back and stared up at the ceiling.

"How could he possibly know the necklace was for Billy's mama?"

A few hours later, I stood outside Rocco's door with three fru-fru coffees plus donuts.

Maria opened the door and crossed herself. "Oh no! Who died?"

"Lots of people, just nobody we know." I pushed the bag of donuts in her hands and followed her through the door to the kitchen.

She looked in the bag. "I'm doing a maple bar before the girls get up."

Maria is super mom. She cooks healthy meals with lots of organic produce. Her home is a sugar-free zone. A woman could crack under the pressure. Once a month we have a standing date. We sneak away for drinks and cheesecake.

"And I'll do an apple fritter," she added.

"Apple is a fruit," I said.

I pulled an old-fashioned donut from the bag.

"Where's Rocco? He's not answering his phone."

"He left early. Captain Bob is all over him about some case he's on. You'll probably find him at the station."

"I'd like to hang around and make some plans with the girls. We have our own trouble to get into when you're in San Francisco."

I opened my bag and gave her two tickets for the Bears/ Giants game. "For Rocco's birthday. I thought you might want to surprise him."

"Rocco said the game was sold out."

"Not for Uncle Joey."

"Wow." She stared at the tickets in her hand. "I hate football."

Captain Bob frowned when I walked into the Ninth Precinct. I should've brought lemon crèmes.

"What are you doing here, Caterina?"

"That hurts, Bob. I'm a professional detective. We're practically colleagues in law enforcement."

A snicker ruptured among some of my colleagues.

"I saw you at the funeral yesterday," Captain Bob said.

"Did you?"

"You walked by and stomped on my foot. And then you kicked your papa on the leg."

"I blame Billy. I seem to be channeling him a lot."

A voice barked from the back. "911. This is Pants On Fire. What is your emergency."

A howl erupted.

"Nice, Leo," I said. "When your wife calls, she's getting a freebie."

"Leo's wife ain't callin'," someone said. "The fire burned out of his pants a long time ago."

"All right, guys," Bob said. "Show's over. Back to work."

I turned to Captain Bob. "Have you found Billy's killer yet?"

"No."

"Because I have the address."

The twitch was back. "Let it go, Caterina. Tierney's not the guy."

"Why do you say that?"

"Because he has no motive and an airtight alibi."

"What if I told you Billy was hot on the trail of a sting that involved Marilyn Monroe and a pair of diamond earrings."

"Oh Jesus. You got hit in the head again, didn't you?"

"Twice."

"For the love of God, see a doctor." He walked away shaking his head.

I called after him. "Be nice, Bob. Or I'll cut you out of my baby pictures."

I wandered over to Rocco's desk and spun around in his chair. Someone said he and Jackson had stepped out on official police business. The guys were back in five minutes with a white bakery bag.

Rocco hugged me. "That was an insane entrance at the funeral yesterday."

"At least I got Billy's St. Christopher necklace back for his mama."

"How'd you convince the women to give it to you?"

"I didn't."

"In and out?"

"Like a ninja."

Rocco picked a jelly donut from the bag and offered me one.

"I'm good. I dropped by your house this morning. Maria said you left early."

Rocco thumped the file on his desk with a fist. "More kicks and giggles from the Bridgeport Bandit. I'm glad you're not working with these guys. We'd never find them."

"What have you got?"

Jackson said, "It's possible the Bridgeport Bandit isn't local. He drives in from Wisconsin, loads up, and goes home."

"That's Jackson's theory," Rocco said.

"Based on hard evidence," Jackson said.

Rocco said, "A Brewers baseball ticket was found on the floor in one of the houses they hit. Owner said it wasn't his."

Jackson said, "It's more than a theory. A guy lives in Chicago, he's a Cubs or Sox fan."

Rocco grunted. "Like I said, it's a theory. What brings you by?"

"It's about the St. Christopher. When I went to the strip poker house, I didn't even say Billy's name. They said they didn't know him."

"They're covering their butts," Rocco said.

I grabbed a tissue and wiped a blob of jelly from my brother's white shirt. "The guy said I should buy my friend's mama another necklace. She wouldn't know the difference."

"And you think she would," Jackson said.

Jackson wasn't paying attention. He placed donuts on a paper plate, practically fondling each one. His eyes had a sugary glaze. I decided I never want to see Savino look at another woman that way.

I said, "How did he know the necklace was for Billy's mama?"

Rocco shrugged. "It's no secret Billy's dead."

"Then why not say, buy another St. Christopher for his *family*. Or the *parents*. I'm telling you, the guy *knew* it was for Billy's mother."

"So Billy told the women he lives with his mother."

"*Really?* Billy's hitting on two gorgeous women and talking about his mama?"

Jackson cut in. "You're making too much of this. Two women drink too much. They pick up Billy and take him home for a threesome."

"This is already hard to swallow," Rocco said.

"Okay," Jackson said, "The husband comes home. The women have sobered up enough to remember one of 'em is married. They panic and throw Billy out the window."

"Except they're not married. Two women, one man, separate bedrooms."

Rocco said, "I checked for any police or incident reports associated with that address. Zip. Nada. Billy's the only one."

"Only what?" I said.

"The only guy who came out of that house in a sock and his shorts."

"And your point?"

Rocco shrugged. "This is a case of booze, sex, and a blatant lack of good sense. Nothing more. I'm sorry, sis. But that was Billy's M.O."

"You're talking about the last time you saw Billy. Eleven years ago. That's the M.O. of every nineteen-year-old guy."

Rocco clearly remembers being nineteen. He didn't argue. "Okay. The two women and the guy. I'll run their names. Maybe something will come up."

"Uh, I don't have names."

"Their license plates?"

I winced. "That's another big zip."

Jackson grinned. "Let me get this straight, Sherlock. You broke into their house, you wandered around, maybe made yourself a sandwich, and you didn't get names or anything for identification?"

"I'll get back to you on that."

"Let it go, sis. It's over. Billy's gone."

"It'll be over when you arrest Kyle Tierney. And I want to be there. If you let me put the cuffs on him, I'll do your laundry for a year."

"You gotta do better than that. Maria already does my laundry."

"You can do my laundry," Jackson winked.

Rocco hung an arm around me and half pushed me outside. I had a feeling he was trying to get rid of me.

"Cat, we've been over this before. You do realize you can't arrest people, don't you? We're not technically colleagues in law enforcement."

"So what are you saying, Rocco?"

"Go home. Catch yourself some cheaters. No one is better at it. Take your pictures. Sweeten some divorce settlements."

I stomped a foot. "I'm not a hootchie stalker. I'm a detective, dammit."

"I know. But leave the arrests and the handcuffing to us. Jackson and I will handle the murder investigation. We'll shoot the bad guys."

"Are you going to shoot Tierney?"

"No."

I kissed his cheek. "Well, then what good are you?"

Chapter Twenty-seven

The obituary for Alan Mitchell was in the *Chicago Sun Times* archives. It took less than five minutes to bring it up.

Mitchell was thirty years old when he was murdered. Graduating from Lake View High School in Ravenswood; he attended night classes at Truman College. He was mostly known by his stage name, Alekazzam the Magnificent. He amazed children and adults with his magic acts.

Unfortunately his last act was less than amazing. It got him killed.

I skimmed past the list of family *survived bys* and *proceeded in death by*. The Benson Family Funeral Home made the arrangements. The service was held at Ravenswood Covenant Church where Mitchell once sang in the choir. The body was interred at Mt. Carmel Cemetery.

That's what I wanted to know.

I looked at Inga and she bolted off for her leash. I grabbed my bag and keys and opened the door.

"Let's find some flowers." And I swung by the Flower Cottage on West 31st.

I bought a fat bouquet of roses, delphinium, and lilies. Then I browsed around the reflective metal yard art section. With apologies to St. Francis, I picked up a cheesy likeness of the saint with a bird blinking on his shoulder. I hit the Dan Ryan, cut over to the Ike, exiting left toward the West Suburbs to 1400 South

Wolf Road. Home to Al Capone, Machine Gun Jack, Bloody Angelo, and a slew of other Chicago gangsters. The home to archbishops, cardinals, and priests. Sinners and saints.

And to Alan Mitchell. Like the rest of us, he was a little bit of both.

We rolled through the iron gate past a couple guys digging a fresh grave. The sod layer had been removed and set aside. A backhoe had done the grunt work. The guys were finishing it off with shovels.

I followed signs to a Chapel and adjoining office. A man who'd outlived most of the residents gave me a map and directions to Mitchell's grave.

I said a prayer for Alan and placed the flowers on his grave. Then I anchored Rudolph St. Francis in the ground. With a little luck, the flashing bird would go unnoticed until we returned later that night.

Cemeteries have rules that protect the dignity of their guests.

I must've been inspired by the cemetery's gorgeous gardens. When I got home, I hung up the new birdfeeder, hoping to attract cardinals. It was certain to fatten the squirrels. I did some weeding in the backyard, cut back the rose bush, and covered the flower beds with a soft bed of mulch for winter.

I was finishing up when Inga bayed out a sound that said, *Alarm! Alarm!*

That could mean anything. Being late for dinner can send panic through a beagle.

I glanced at my watch. Mama gave her an early afternoon snack about now.

I said, "Are you hungry, girl?"

She screamed again, hair up on her back.

"Me too. Let's find something to eat."

I scooped my tools in the bucket and hopped on the porch behind Inga. I grabbed the door knob. It wouldn't turn. The door was locked, bolted from the inside. Someone was inside my house.

I grasped for my phone. I needed to call any DeLuca with a badge and a gun that wasn't defending underwear. My hand trembled and came up empty. The cell was in my bag on the little table by the door.

Did I lock the front door when I came in? I didn't remember. But apparently an alarm doesn't go off if you don't set it.

I pressed my face to the window. A flash of tall and skinny wooshed down the hall in a black face mask.

Devin!

I would wring his scrawny neck.

I was too mad to be scared. I seized my garden hoe and broke a small glass window pane on the door. I reached my hand inside and unlocked the dead bolt. That was too easy. Instead of replacing the broken one, I made a mental note to replace every pane with unbreakable glass.

I told Inga to wait outside. I didn't want her to see me clobber her new best sausage-friend.

I turned the knob and kicked the door open like Rambo.

"I saw you, Devin, you weasely little man. Come out before I call the cops."

I stomped through the kitchen and down the hall to my bedroom.

"I'm getting my gun, Devin," I yelled. "If you're smart you'll be gone before I—"

My hand jerked open the drawer, ruffling Victoria's Secrets. There was a sound behind me.

I whirled to face the black mask, pistol cocked, silk and lace entwined in my fingers.

Fifty-thousand volts went through me. My legs dissolved to Jell-o. I crashed. The nightstand broke my fall. When I opened my eyes again, my forehead had a sticky new bump. My hand clutched the panties.

And my 9mm Glock was gone.

Chapter Twenty-eight

I washed off the blood from the nasty bump on my forehead with hydrogen peroxide. It was a doozy. There would be no concealing this one with make-up. I found scissors and gave myself bangs.

I counted to twenty. Ten doesn't cut it with Devin. Then I took two aspirin and told myself I couldn't kill Devin with my bare hands. I wasn't convinced.

I changed into a long-sleeved hoodie and threw on a pair of Nike pants and bombed over to Jack's shop. Devin would be expecting me. I wondered if he'd have the courage to show up.

Jack was in his office when I stomped in.

"Caterina."

"Stay out of this, Jack. I'm coming for Devin."

"What did he do now?"

"Forty-five minutes ago he broke in my house. He knocked me out and took my 9mm."

"That's not possible."

"The guy's crazy, Jack," I shrieked. "He's got a *gun*."

Jack opened the inside door to the shop. "Devin. Can I see you a minute."

I didn't wait five seconds. I charged past his uncle, into the shop.

"Devin, show yourself, you miserable coward."

It sounded a bit like I was calling him out for a wild-west showdown. Except Devin had my gun.

The weasel poked his head out from under a hood. "Hey, Cat. What's up?"

"You just broke in my house, dirtbag."

He sniffed. "Huh?"

"You stole my gun. You gave me *this*." I swept my hair back, exposing the wound.

"Ouch," Jack said.

My teeth wouldn't unclench. "*I. Hate. Bangs.*"

Devin shrugged. "It wasn't me. I was here."

"Liar!"

Jack walked over to a time sheet on the wall. "Since eight this morning."

He did the finger-circle thing around his ear and jerked his head at me.

"I'm not crazy," I snapped. "I saw him."

"You couldn't, ma'am," a southern voice drawled. "Devin was here with me. We're rebuilding this engine together."

It was Irene's husband from the Marco Polo. Colby's dad. There was an alarmed look in his eyes. He wasn't going to let the crazy woman near his son anytime soon.

Devin wheezed. "Like he said, Cat. I was here all bloody day."

When we were kids, Devin used to say his Indian name was *He who snots a lot.* His sinuses are his tell. He wheezes.

I realized, at that moment, that the masked figure in my bedroom didn't.

I needed to get out of Bridgeport for a while. Somewhere where people didn't know me well enough to think I was crazy.

I changed into sweats and running shoes and my partner and I drove to the North Shore. I pounded the pavement hard, panting and exorcizing Devin from my shoulders.

I breathed in the lake and the gorgeous Chicago skyline. Chicago is a runner's paradise. The annual North Shore half marathon draws four thousand participants each year. Max is one of them. He wants me to join him next year. I dunno. I do my best running when bad guys are chasing me. I find I'm more inspired that way.

The rigid discipline and commitment for training that marathons require is daunting, to say the least. But I promised Max I'd think about it. And I'll think about it again on my way home, right after we stop for ice cream.

I returned home, feeling balanced and much more relaxed. I took a shower, checked my emails, and hit the road for Cleo's to help set up for Mrs. Millani's bridge party.

Cleo thought of everything. We loaded the Camry with a tantalizing assortment of appetizers, shortbread decorated like playing cards, and fruity Sangria. She even added hot wings in memory of Billy.

We arrived at the Millani home an hour early, just behind Mama and her Italian cream cake. She wore a new red-and-white-print dress and patent leather, black mary janes that showed off her raven black hair. Mama is never late to a social event. She's the eyes and ears of Bridgeport. People depend on her for advice and the latest gossip.

"We don't live by Ciabatta alone," Mama states with every juicy tidbit.

We set up the party in the gazebo off the patio. When we were kids, Becky and I helped her dad build it. We had some of our best Nancy Drew adventures there. She has her own family now, and we're not as close as we once were. We don't have a lot in common anymore.

Becky was in the kitchen fixing her three year old a snack of grapes and cheese. She looked exhausted and pale. Evan clung to her jeans crying. He had a snotty nose.

Mrs. Millani picked him up and he stopped. She said, "Becky and Tom are expecting a second baby in the spring." She beamed. "It will be our first granddaughter."

"Wow, a girl," I said. "Congratulations."

I went to hug her and tripped over Evan's fire truck.

Mama pulled a tissue from her bra and dabbed an eye. "You must be proud to have a daughter who gives you grandchildren."

Becky looked like she was going to throw up.

"You have Sophie," I reminded her. "The walking baby factory."

Mama fanned the tissue out and blew.

I changed the subject. "I didn't see you at Billy's funeral, Becky."

She made a face. "Evan got sick at the last minute. I couldn't take him to the sitter's."

I filled her in on who was there and how our high school friends have changed in the last decade.

"Remember Danno's long hair?"

She closed her eyes. "I'm seeing Jesus."

"I'm seeing Charles Manson. Anyway, the hair's almost gone."

"Can't picture him in a buzz cut."

"Balding. Big time. He parts what he has left over his ear and does a comb over. It *so* doesn't work."

She laughed. "It never does."

"Remember that little nerdy guy in chemistry? Everyone wanted to sit by him and copy his answers."

She laughed. "That was just you. His name is Lee."

"Remember the senior prom? He must have asked a hundred girls. And still didn't get a date."

"Well, he wasn't afraid of being turned down."

"Lee's not having trouble getting the ladies anymore."

Her mouth dropped. "He's gorgeous?"

"Nerdier than ever."

"Rich?"

"Filthy. And still playing with his chemistry set. Lee's company builds weapons of mass destruction for the military."

"That's scary."

"That's what I thought," I said. "We're all getting together next week for Billy. Maybe bring pictures and get something to eat. I can pick you up, if you'd like, and we'll go together."

"I'd love to. Let me know when and I'll try to get away."

"Of course you can go," Becky's mom said. "I'll take Evan for the night."

Becky gave her first broad smile. "Honestly, I wouldn't trade my life with anyone. But there are definitely some things you miss when you have kids." She laughed. " Like going out. And sleeping in."

Mama fixed a practiced eye of mother guilt on me. "And there are definitely things you miss when you *don't* have kids."

I mostly miss the morning sickness. And, of course, the joy of labor.

"I still have time, Mama. I'm not dead yet."

"You're thirty, Caterina. Your pipes are rusting."

"Who has rusty pipes?" Ken Millani walked in hearing dollar signs. "I'll take a look at them."

"They're not the kind of pipes you can fix, dear," his wife said.

Ken gave hugs around. Evan squirmed out of grandma's arms and into grandpa's.

"Can't stay," Ken said. "I saw Becky's car and stopped by for a tickle."

He wiggled his fingers at Evan's belly and the toddler squealed.

"Stick around," Becky said. "Mama's having her bridge club over."

He kissed his daughter's cheek. "Why do you think I'm running?"

Ken handed his grandson to his mom and turned to me.

"When can I put that other floor on your house, Cat? You need to marry that nice FBI agent. It's too nice a house to not fill with children."

"From your lips to God's ears," Mama did the sign of the cross and breathed.

Becky kicked her dad.

Ken's eyes twinkled. *"What?"*

I threw Evan's fire truck at him, and he ducked out the door laughing.

Chapter Twenty-nine

The night was cold and clear. A full moon hung over Chicago. I wore Billy's Philip Marlowe coat to the cemetery. The coat was baggy and his belt wrapped around me twice. I liked to think Billy was with us when we found Marilyn's diamond earrings.

Max obliterated the night padlock on the cemetery gate. He cut the headlights and closed the gate behind us.

Navigating by moonlight, we followed the map the old man gave me earlier that day. We drove by countless statues to the Holy Mother and to the angels and blessed saints. But only one bird flickered in the night like a neon beer sign. It pulled us in.

Max cut the engine and the four of us tumbled out of the Hummer and grabbed a shovel from the back. Alan's tear-shaped marker had a carving of Mother Mary. Fresh flowers burst from a vase shaped as a magician's hat. Alan's parents spared no expense saying good bye to their son.

The four of us stood over Alan Mitchell's grave. I don't know what the others were thinking. But there I was, in the company of Al Capone and Bugs Moran and the ghosts of the mafia from days gone by. I, for one, was thinking, *move over, guys. I am so going to hell for this.*

I cut a sideways glance at Cristina. She was chewing her lip. She really didn't get the cause and effect thing. She took no responsibility for her part in Mitchell's death. Mostly she looked as if she was going to be sick. The last time she saw Alan

Mitchell he was freshly dead. She really didn't want to see how he looks now.

The ground was cold and hard. My breathing was labored and my shoulders ached. Max hadn't broken a sweat. He swung a shovel as effortlessly as a child in a sandbox. Cleo groaned with each scoop. Women have given birth with less theatrics.

"Try taking bigger shovelfuls," Cristina sang from her perch on a tombstone.

Cleo gasped for breath. "If there's room in that casket, she's going in."

Cristina shuddered. "Remember those ghost stories we told when we were kids? There's always a cemetery at night under a full moon."

I glanced at the sky. When I looked down again, Cristina was beside me. Her nails dug deep into my hand.

"Something moved out there. Did you see it?"

"That's gonna leave a mark," I said prying her fingers loose. "And yes, I saw the possum."

"It had horrible yellow eyes," she whispered shrilly. "It was four feet tall."

"Ghosts don't have yellow eyes," Cleo said wisely. "Zombies do."

Cristina trembled.

I heard Max smile. "Relax, you're putting yourselves into your own frightmare. There's no such thing as ghosts."

"Next he'll be telling us there's no Easter Bunny," I said.

Cristina wrapped her arms around herself. "I didn't know this would be dangerous."

Max said, "You're in a cemetery under a full moon. You're digging up a corpse and robbing his grave. I can't speak for the Pope, but Lutherans go to hell for this."

"How's that for dangerous?" Cleo winked.

"What if we're caught?" Cristina whined.

I did some calculating. "If the boys in blue appear, it'll cost a night in jail, a stiff fine, long humiliating hours of community service, and a court appointed psychiatric evaluation."

Cristina said, "I can fake crazy real well. Just sayin'."

Cleo said, "If Cristina doesn't start shoveling, we snag the earrings, smash her head with a shovel, and bury her in the coffin with her friend."

"My lips are sealed," Max said.

"I'm in this for Billy," I said. "Suit yourselves."

Cristina made a little whimper and picked up her shovel.

When I was pretty sure my arms were falling off, I took a break. I walked over to the Hummer where Cleo had set up Tino's moonlight supper. There was enough food to raise the dead. I chose a turkey sandwich, Italian cookies, and a flask of hot coffee. And a few of my Oreo cookies.

I wandered a bit with my flashlight and ate my supper with the bones of Harry Bengston. Harry was a casualty of war. He died in Korea before my parents were born.

I listened to the stillness around me. Occasional hum of passing cars but the bones were at rest. No sound in the air but the schiff-chuff of our shovels and the flying globs of earth landing on a pile.

Our hearty dig to China.

I set out a sandwich and two cookies for the possum. When I reached for my shovel again, a scruff in the darkness turned my blood cold. I signaled the others to listen. There it was again. A rustle of dead leaves. A boot, perhaps, brushing against a stone. I didn't know about the others, but I hoped it was Harry getting some air.

"Yellow eyes," Cristina whispered hoarsely.

"The cops are here," Max said. "Busted."

"They don't have us yet." Cleo patted her pockets wildly. "My gun. I don't have my gun."

Cleo's not having a gun is always a good thing.

"It's okay," I said. "You're not going to shoot your way out of a cemetery."

Cristina wielded her shovel like a weapon. "Show your yellow eyes."

"She's not going to do well with the psychiatric evaluation," Max said.

"Someone stole my freakin' gun," Cleo shrieked.

"Neither will Cleo," he said.

"Who's there?" I called.

A muffled voice shot out of the darkness. "Chicago Police. You are under arrest. Lay down your weapons and raise your hands above your heads."

Cleo complied. Cristina's hands shot up. Max and I looked at each other.

"Do something, Cat," Cleo said furiously. "Jail sucks."

"You would know," Max said.

I held onto my shovel. "Show yourself. We have no reason to drop anything until we see your identification."

"You go, girl," Cleo cheered reaching for the stars.

"Here's a reason. There's a small cannon directed at your face."

"That'll do." I dropped the shovel like a hot potato and my hands grasped at a big, yellow moon.

Frankie stepped from the shadows. Cleo howled and everyone laughed but me.

I looked at Max, still holding his shovel.

"He wasn't scary enough," he said.

"He's crazy enough. You weren't concerned about the cannon?"

Max shrugged. "He said it was small. Mine is bigger."

I smiled. "Bummer for Cleo."

Frankie tromped over all macho-like and reached for my shovel. "Take a break, girls. The guys got this."

I defended the metal in my hands like mama's cannoli recipe. "I hope you brought your own."

He stripped the shovel from my hands. "Yours is warm already."

Frankie winked at Cleo, and plunged the shovel deep into the earth with unrelenting vigor.

"Frankie has stamina," Cleo sighed.

"That's something," I said.

I worked my biceps dunking Oreos in hot coffee. We measured their progress as body parts sank from sight. They were deep in the hole with piles of dirt on both sides, dark heads dropping from view when the clank of metal on metal caught my breath.

"We're at the casket," Max called.

"Yee haw!" Cleo said.

Oreos scattered and we raced to cheer them on. Cristina crossed her fingers. "We'll soon know if Alan took the earrings with him."

Cleo glanced around uneasily. "Do you suppose he's watching?"

Cristina looked around for yellow eyes. "Who?"

"You know who," Cleo flicked her head toward the casket. "I hope he's not mad at us for being here."

I spelled it out for Cristina. "Cleo wonders if Alan Mitchell knows we're out here in the middle of the night, stomping the shit out of his daisies, tossing him about like a jack-in-the-box, and robbing his grave. And if he knows, does he care?"

Cristina leaned over the hole and spoke slowly in a really loud voice. "This is all Cat's fault."

"I'm sure he heard that," I said.

I know the neighbors did.

"Do you really think so?"

Cristina didn't want to know what I really thought. I'd spent two hours in a cemetery under a full moon, something no reasonably sane person would do. I was getting punchy. Catholic voices from my childhood warned me that desecrating the dead is one of those go-directly-to-hell-do-not-pass-go kinds of sins. While this wasn't the only unpardonable sin I've committed, it could be the first that didn't involve alcohol.

Shovels jammed the earth. Dirt flew. Finally the guys stood before a once-shiny silver box.

"It's a casket alright," my rocket-scientist cousin announced.

Max placed his hands under the lid. "Drum roll, please."

We didn't breathe. Slowly, the coffin opened.

And so it was that a glorious moon was to shine on Alan Mitchell once again, four years after his death.

We leaned over the hole and flashed a light inside. Dark, eyes sockets stared back at us. Boney fingers clasped over his chest.

Cristina covered her face with her hands and shuddered. "Poor Alan."

"Eeuuuw," Cleo said. "I'm going for cremation."

Frankie flashed a light in the box. He shrugged. "I don't see no diamonds."

"Mitchell swallowed them." I crossed my fingers. "Look in his stomach."

I blinked and Frankie stood beside me. He was staring at me. "*You* look in his stomach."

Max held up his arms. "C'mon, Bogie. I'll catch you."

I tossed my flashlight down and sat on the grassy edge, my legs dangling. Max put his hands around my waist and lifted me down to the ground. He held me there a moment.

He whispered in my ear. "I'm seeing you naked under that trench coat."

"In your dreams."

I placed my hands on the sides of his head, as if reading his mind.

"That's not me. Those giant melons aren't mine."

He grinned. "They're Marilyn's. But the rest is you."

I lightly smacked the side of his head and picked up the flashlight.

"Hello, Alan." Taking a deep, steadying breath, I carefully explored the remains with my hands. When I spoke, my voice was bleak. I said. "The earrings aren't here."

"Look again," Cristina demanded.

Max dropped an arm around me, his hand cupping my shoulder. "It was smart detective work, Kitten. And you were right about the diamonds. Mitchell should have swallowed them."

"Only he didn't."

Cleo said, "Someone has a fat retirement plan tucked in a drawer with his socks."

"Or pantyhose," Cristina said.

"If I was da first responder, I wouldn't be drivin' dat piece of shit Pontiac," Frankie said.

"You'd look fine in a Ferrari," Cleo said. "Like your Uncle Joey."

"Hell yeah," Frankie said.

"I'll pass that on to Kyle Tierney. He's sure to understand."

Max said, "If you let me handle Tierney, you won't hear from him again."

"Neither will anyone else." I made a face. "Thanks, but I have to figure this out on my own."

"We're done here," Frankie said. "Cleo and I will meet you at Mickeys. Cat's buying."

I murmured something to Mitchell and was straightening his tie when my hand brushed his Adam's apple. It was a honker.

"Gimme some light," I said.

Max beamed the flashlight. The eerie, vacant eye sockets stared back at me.

"Did your friend have a protruding Adam's apple?" I asked Cristina.

"Not that I recall."

"You'd remember this one."

A giddy grin spread across my face. It was another stickler. I elbowed Max. "What do you think?"

I think maybe a bullet saved this guy from choking to death.

I shut my eyes for a moment and murmured an apology to Alan Mitchell. Another to all the saints. To every nun and priest who tried to make me the kind of person who doesn't desecrate graves and rip open a dead guy's throat. But mostly to Mama. She scares me more than all the others combined.

I braced myself. This was going to be hell at the confessional.

I gently worked the leathery neck with my fingertips. The skin was paper thin. It parted with the lightest touch. The Adam's apple fell away and diamonds—as pure as water—dazzled in the light.

No scalpel. No Dr. Frankenstein. I hoped the saints took notice.

"Damn, girl," Max breathed.

I removed them carefully and cupped the chandelier earrings in my hands. They were identical round cuts. Each a perfect carat. They took my breath away.

Frankie whistled low. "Who says you can't take it with you?"

Cristina dropped a hand down. "We wanna see. I'll hold them for you."

I gave her the earrings and straightened Mitchell's tie one more time.

"Thank you," I whispered.

Max closed the casket. He put his hands around my waist. "I'll lift you up."

"Stop," Cristina said. "Stay where you are."

There was something in her voice—less sinister than whacko. My heart dropped in my chest.

Cleo screeched. "Is that my gun? You stole my freakin' gun."

"Don't get your panties in a bunch. You'll get it back."

"And I'll pop you with it."

Frankie growled. "I'll kill her."

"Stand in line," Max said.

Cristina said, "Those earrings belong to me. I'm taking them with me."

"Hello, village idiot, the diamonds belong to Marilyn's estate," I said.

"Uh—whatever, freak girl." The moon lit her deranged smile. "I'll just need to borrow Max's Hummer."

Big mistake.

"Oh boy," I said.

With a single cat-like leap, Max surged to the surface and tackled the woman waving Cleo's gun.

The diamonds flew from Cristina's hands, shimmering in the night. Cleo took a dive that would have made any pro running back proud, capturing the earrings in midflight. She landed hard, crashing and burning into Harry's tombstone. She came up with the diamonds clenched in a fist, arm extended high, they never touched the ground.

Max hoisted me up. "No one messes with my rig."

I looked at Cristina. Her head was resting on Alan's marker. She was out cold.

"Yo, Max," Frankie said. "She had a freakin' gun on us. You know, it cudda gone off."

Max shook his head. "The safety was on."

"Sheesh! Amateur hour." Cleo clobbered Cristina with her shovel. "That's for stealing my gun."

"Yeah," Frankie said and kicked her.

"She's already out," Max said. "She can't feel that."

"She will." Cleo wrestled her pocket and whipped out a stun gun at Cristina.

Zzzzzzzzzzap

Cristina moaned and opened panicked eyes.

Cleo lifted the taser to her lips and blew. "That's for messing with my gun."

Cleo looked at Cristina. She looked down at the hole.

I said, "No."

"Bummer," Cleo said.

Cristina sat up and cradled her head. There was an angry red mark on her forehead and a sticky trickle of blood down the side of her face.

"I need to get a few band aids in my bag," Cristina said.

"Move and I'll cap your sorry ass. Band aids won't do you much good then." Frankie's cheerful voice was terrifying.

I said a prayer for Alan Mitchell and tossed the flowers I bought at the Flower Cottage in his grave. We refilled the hole and rolled the sod back over the dirt.

Cleo packed away her moonlit supper. We stashed the shovels in the back with the bolt cutters and the padlock from the cemetery gate. Cristina climbed into the backseat. Cleo jerked her out.

"Uh uh, crazy cakes. You walk."

"Don't look at me," Frankie said. "Lunatic Barbie ain't ridin' with me."

Cristina threw her big doe eyes at Max. "*Please*, Max." Blink blink.

"Really?" I said.

"Nobody steals my Hummer and expects a ride."

"Cat! *Help!*" she whimpered.

"You should walk to California," I said reasonably. "But the adults here have to think about Halah Rose."

"Who?" Cleo said.

"Dammit," Max said. "All right. Cristina rides in the Hummer. But she goes home tomorrow."

Cristina tapped her chin. "I'll need a couple days to put some things together."

"Can't we just shoot her?" Cleo said.

"Yes," I said.

We all loaded in the Hummer and cruised to the gate. Cristina was quiet in the back between Cleo and Frankie. I didn't have to look over my shoulder to know Cleo's taser was on her lap. And her fingers were twitching.

Max drove to the entrance and stepped outside to open the big, black iron gate.

I swirled the diamonds in the palm of my hand and watched them catch the moon.

There was a scuffle by the gate. Instinctively I dropped the earrings in a pocket. A man emerged from the shadows, looming up suddenly and charging at Max. The figure went at him head-down, bull-like, ramming into his back. They hit the ground hard. Max recovered quickly and with a few angry twists and slugs, was on top of his attacker. Max punched him in the solar plexus. The air went out of his lungs with a loud whoosh.

Max dragged him to his feet and snapped him around into a choke hold. The man made strangled, gasping sounds, like a wounded animal.

I shot out of the Hummer and rubbed my eyes. "Garret?"

"You know this creep?"

I blinked, stunned. "He's the ex-fiancé I was telling you about—"

A pistol jammed against my head.

"And here's the fox-killing dramapocaylpse now," I said.

"Watch yourself," Sylvia said. "Let him go. Or I'll blow her pretty little brain into itty bitty bits."

Max released Garret's throat. Garret pulled a Beretta from his shoulder holster and trained it on Max.

"Stay where you are, Rambo," Garret choked.

"Pussy," Max spat. "I should've broken your neck."

Garret walked around the Hummer and loosened the valve core on all four tires. The air whistled, and the tires went flat.

"Now you pissed me off," Max said.

"You'll regret that," I smiled.

"Bite me." Garret growled.

"I'll take those earrings now," Sylvia said.

"Give them to her, Kitten," Max said.

I dropped a hand in my pocket.

"No!" Cristina screamed. "Don't do it!"

"Seriously?"

Sylvia said, "You got five seconds. Earrings in my hand or I shoot the big mouth in the backseat."

"Would you?" Cleo said.

I pulled the baubles from my pocket and threw them at her. She scooped them off the ground, laughing.

"Thanks," she said.

"Go to hell," Cleo said.

"How did you know we'd be here?" I said.

"They've been following us for days," Cleo said.

Sylvia gave a hard laugh. "We didn't have to."

I mentally backtracked. "When you came to my house, you planted a bug, didn't you?"

"That's creepy," Cleo said.

"You're a monster," Cristina shrieked. "You got no heart."

Sylvia laughed. "Now that's something I used to hear every day."

They scooted out the gate backward, wielding their pistols like Bonny and Clyde. Max jerked his door open and would have torn after them, but I pulled him back.

"Wait," I whispered.

"You're not going to let them get away with this?" Cleo demanded indignantly.

"Cowards," Cristina screamed into the night.

Frankie and Cleo brandished weapons. "What are we waiting for?"

On the other side of the gate, a motorcycle kicked into gear and roared into the night.

"Let them go," I said. "They got nothin'."

"My diamonds," Cristina wailed.

"Shut up," Cleo said and zapped her.

I ducked my hand in a pocket and pulled out Marilyn's earrings.

Cleo stammered. "But you gave her—"

"The ones from the crime photos. They're a perfect costume copy. But worthless. Mitchell pulled a switch on Tierney. It got him killed."

Cleo smacked my shoulder with unabashed admiration. "You *stole* those from police evidence?"

"*Borrowed.* I can buy a replacement online for under a hundred dollars."

"You'll get your money back," Max said grimly. "I'll take a lot more out of that dirtbag's hide when I find him."

"I parked behind the bike when I came in," Frankie said.

"Did you get the license?"

"No, dammit. But the plates were out of state."

Max fired up the Hummer and coaxed the flattened tires through the iron gate. He parked on the street behind Frankie's Pontiac.

I heard Max's teeth grind. "I'll find that dumbshit. He left fingerprints all over my rig when he flattened the tires."

"Yeah," Frankie growled all macho. "We'll hunt his sorry ass down."

I kissed Max's cheek. "That won't be necessary. Sylvia told us who she is."

Max rubbernecked. "What did I miss?"

"She said she has no heart. She's the Tin Woman."

"Tin Woman?"

Cleo gave a hoot. "She's Nicole Bonham. Billy's bitch-of-a-wife."

I smiled broadly. "And the plates were Kansas."

Chapter Thirty

It should've been embarrassing having to call Chance to Al Capone's burial place in the middle of the night for a ride. We were a motley bunch. Filthy, sweaty, all dressed in black—me draped in Billy's honkin' huge Philip Marlowe coat. Frankly, I was too tired to care.

We were huddled outside the Hummer when Chance's Toyota Highlander pulled up.

He climbed out, saw Max. His brow rose.

"Max?"

"Chance," Max said, and climbed into the backseat.

Chance frowned. "What's he doing here?"

I shrugged.

Cleo threw her arms around Chance. "I could kiss you," she said and did. "I'm freezing my ass off out here."

"*Muchas gracias*," Cristina said and climbed in the car with Max.

Chance said, "That must be Cristina from California. Why's she bleeding."

"I know, huh?" Cleo said. "I wanted to stuff her in the coffin. But no!"

Chance's jaw dropped. "Coffin?"

I drew a circle in the air, pointing at my ear. Like Cleo was crazy. It's not a hard sell.

"Yo, thanks for the lift, man," Frankie said. "I dropped my keys in the casket."

Chance shot me a look.

"All right," I admitted. "But there was just the one."

Frankie climbed into the backseat and Cleo wriggled onto his lap. She giggled.

Chance smiled. "That's a new look for you, Inspector Clouseau."

"It's Phyllis Marlowe. I've been channeling Billy a lot."

"You're not serious."

"Yep."

"Tell me it wasn't when we were making love." Our eyes locked for a brief moment.

I ran my fingers around the back of his neck, leaned in, and whispered softly in his ear. "Take me home, big boy. You're going to love the reindeer boxers."

◇◇◇

Chance was due in court early. When the phone woke me at eight, he was gone and I smelled coffee.

I could get used to this.

I reached for the phone without opening my eyes. Uncle Joey didn't wait for me to speak.

"Tell me."

"Yes."

He laughed.

"Uncle Joey? Uh, hello?"

He was gone.

I padded to the kitchen and opened the secret compartment behind the pantry. Marilyn's diamonds sparkled beside some dusty bottles of moonshine left over from Prohibition. I cupped the earrings in my hand and sat at the table with my coffee and the morning paper. Even the editorial about political unrest in Washington seemed cheerier with the dazzling diamonds in the corner of my eye.

I called Cleo and asked her to meet me at my house. "There's something I want to check out."

"You're not gonna wear Billy's coat again, are you? Cuz every time I see it, I wanna zap Cristina."

"No coat. Where is she now?"

"In bed."

Probably hiding from the taser.

"Bring her with you."

Cleo snorted. "Well, duh. I'm not leaving psycho-belle here with the silver."

"Mama's taking Halah and Inga and Beau to a concert at Archer Park. She'll drop them at my house later."

"I'm pulling pastries from the oven," Cleo said. "We'll eat them at your house."

"No rat poison in Cristina," I reminded her. "She has a daughter."

"I know, dammit."

Uncle Joey burst through the door out of breath. "Where are they?"

"Gotta go," I said and disconnected.

I kissed his cheek and dropped the diamonds in his hand. Uncle Joey closed his eyes and sighed deeply.

"I can smell her."

I laughed. "You and your obsession with Marilyn."

His eyes began to twinkle. "What man isn't?"

He fondled the earrings at the table, and I poured coffee in his favorite mug. Cleo and Cristina arrived a few minutes later with a platter of warm Crostatas. She had filled the dense, buttery crusts with sour cherry and apricot jam.

Already in a weakened state, Uncle Joey almost dropped to his knees.

Cristina had pancaked on the makeup. Her bruises from last night's unfortunate encounter with a tombstone were still visible. She seemed anxious to make amends. She did up the dishes.

Cristina talked about Bridgeport and her time working at the Irish Pub.

"I hope you can stick around a while," Uncle Joey said. "Linda's parents are friends with a guy who plays bass in the symphony. I know he'd take Halah to a rehearsal and introduce her to—"

"No!" I fairly screamed and checked the panic from my voice. "Uhm, they're going home tomorrow. Halah's hoping to make her school concert."

Uncle Joey said, "Where do you live?"

"Far, far away," I said.

Uncle Joey gave me a strange look I pretended not to notice.

After a while he said, "I contacted the studio and the insurance company this morning. I informed them the *Some Like It Hot* earrings have been found."

Cristina sniffed. "They were happy?"

Cleo snorted. "As happy as you were the thirty seconds you held them in your back-stabbing hand."

Cristina stomped off in a huff. I suspected she wanted distance from Cleo and her zap-happy taser.

Joey looked as if he was going to ask what that was about and then decided he didn't care. He brought the earrings to his face again and smelled the ghost of Marilyn. He set them down gently.

He said, "They cudda kissed me through the phone. The studio is sending a courier out tomorrow. The reward from the studio and the check from the insurance company will be issued once the earrings are authenticated."

Cleo looked giddy. "You're rich, Cat."

"Not exactly. The check from the insurance company will go to Mrs. Bonham. Billy would like that."

"Dammit, Cat," Cleo said. "You're giving it all away? What's wrong with you?"

Uncle Joey groaned. "You're tough on the outside. But inside you're all soft and gooey like this crostata."

"There are worse things to be," I smiled over my coffee cup.

Uncle Joey said, "There's still the reward from the studios. A hundred thousand smackaroos."

I caught my breath. "That's a lot of roo."

Cleo said, "So whatcha gonna do with it?"

"I dunno. I might take a road trip. I'm thinking of going to Kansas. And I might buy a new car."

Joey said, "You love the Silver Bullet."

"Yeah. But Cristina's Subaru will never make it to California. If I don't give her my car, she'll never leave. If she stays, one day I'll flip out and choke the life out of her. I'll have to stuff her body in the trunk and push my car off a pier. Then, I'll have to go to confession. I'll lose my car either way. At least the Silver Bullet has a future in California."

"The winters are nice there," Cleo said.

"That's what I thought."

Uncle Joey winked. "You may want to hold off on the Silver Bullet a while. I might have a car for her."

"Oh?"

"Let's just say I know a guy."

I smiled. "You always do."

◇◇◇

Cleo parked down the street from the house where Billy had lost his last game of strip poker. We were in her Camry. I had questions, and I needed some answers soon. I was running out of cars they wouldn't recognize.

"You think it's a good idea to leave Cristina alone at your house?" Cleo asked.

"Nope. But her Subaru is out of gas and on its last cylinder. Whatever she takes, she'll have to hide under her coat. I hid Marilyn's earrings, my jewelry, my Chihuly vase, my pair of Gucci pumps, and my fav pair of jeans behind the pantry. Anything else I can live without."

"What about that half angel-half devil statuette your sister gave you last Christmas."

I made a face. "It's hideous, isn't it? I taped a $20 dollar bill to it and left it by the door. If Cristina has any compassion, she'll take it."

Cleo lowered the visor and checked her make-up. "You got the St. Christopher. What are we doing here?"

"I think the three of them were spying on Billy."

"Spying on Billy?" Cleo laughed. She stopped when she saw my face. "You're serious."

"Rocco didn't believe me either."

"Because it's a dumb idea."

"Call it a hunch."

"I call it dumb." She freshened her lipstick and closed the visor. "So, what are we looking for."

"I need their names."

"There are easier ways to find out who lives here."

I flashed a smile. "But they're not as much fun. Take the camera. Photograph anything that'll help Joey Jr. with background and financials."

My cousin Joey Jr. is a computer genius. He's also my personal hacker. Joey's in his first year at Harvard. My Uncle Joey is almost done pouting. He could be the only parent in history who's disappointed his son has a full scholarship to Harvard.

I tell him to get over himself.

"Harvard can't beat Notre Dame," Uncle Joey says. "They play in the Ivy league."

"Shut up," I tell him.

He snorts. "There's only two good reasons to go to college. Football and spring break in Cabo."

Cleo pulled her .454 Casull, checked it, and stuffed it back in her shoulder holster.

"You brought a freakishly large gun," I said.

She opened her door. "Yeah, I had this shoulder holster made especially for this big boy. The other one was a bitch on my back. Come on, girlfriend. It's a good day to blast somebody."

The living room was different. The oil painting above the fireplace was a Charles Russell. The scene was an Indian buffalo hunt. Thundering horses, flying arrows, and buffalo stampeding the hell out of Dodge. You don't often see a Charles Russell east of the Mississippi. It was a curious choice for a guy with a Chicago accent and a stack of Judas Priest CDs in his room. Maybe he won it in a poker game. I suspected he wouldn't know buffalo dung if he was standing in it.

Cleo put on her gloves and began to search through cupboards and drawers. She got the names of the women who pushed Billy out a window. Linda Daily and Tasha Blume. They appeared to work for separate insurance companies. Jay Pruitt was the guy who played the husband. There was a picture of him at a White Sox game with friends. Cleo said he looked like Shrek.

I looked for anything that would give more information about the three roommates. The computer files were password protected. I downloaded them all and sent a copy to my email. There was a bag by the door I didn't remember seeing the other day. It was packed for a workout at the gym with one extra feature. A fully loaded .32 magnum tucked in an inside pocket.

I found Cleo in the kitchen drinking chocolate milk. She wiped her lipstick from the carton and offered me a spoon.

"Try the chicken almond casserole. It's amazing."

"Nope, I'm good."

She opened the freezer and poked around. "Cool, dude. This guy has a box of Choco Frozen Puffs. They were the best ever."

"You gonna have one?"

She was eating everything else anyway.

"Nah. They're old. Choco Frozen Puffs went out of business last year. Maybe he's gonna sell that box on eBay."

"Or he never cleans his refrigerator."

The answering machine flashed the number three. I pushed play.

The first message was for Linda. She'd neglected to pick up her dry cleaning.

The next voice was Jay's mother, wondering what time to expect him Saturday.

The last message was a puzzle. A man's voice, and he didn't waste words. "Got your message. Let's see what you got. One-thirty." Click.

I replayed the message.

"What is it?"

I gnawed a lip. "That voice."

Her brow tilted. "Friend or foe?"

"I dunno. But I recognize it. I've heard it recently."

"Think."

I wrinkled my nose and tapped my forehead. "I got nothing." I said, "I wonder what he meant, 'I want to see what you got.'"

"It's a code. Jay Pruitt is a dirty rotten drug dealer."

"And you know this how?"

"I know codes," she said wisely.

"You don't know codes."

Drug dealer? Actually, it made perfect, twisted sense. The spendy furniture, oil paintings, spanking new stainless steel appliances. And the guarded, paranoid behavior when I knocked on their door.

"I almost forgot." Cleo pulled a picture from her pocket and slapped it on the table.

Bill Bonham in his private dick coat, scrunched behind a red maple tree. It was a picture of Billy photographing Coochie, and Will Peterson, and the gold-toothed ogre in the park. My throat went dry.

"Where did you find this?"

"In the closet. In the inside coat pocket."

"They were watching him."

Cleo said, "Here's what happened. The women pick up Billy for a game of strip poker. They steal his wallet. When they discover he's a regular Philip Marlowe, they get worried. Like maybe he's investigating them." She took another spoonful of casserole. "Poor ol' Billy just wanted to get laid."

"So they follow him?"

"I agree they'd have to have some big freakin' secrets."

"Well, Phyllis Marlowe. There's a problem with your theory."

I scooted the photo across the table. She brought it close to her face and scrunched her nose. When the light bulb went on, she got bug-eyed.

"The St. Christopher. He's wearing it."

"Excellent, Watson. The photograph was taken *before* they played strip poker."

"So the women didn't randomly pick him up at the bar."

"No. They followed him there."

"Why?"

"I don't know yet. But it has something to do with a nasty divorce, two men in a park, and a little white dog."

Cleo stared hard at the photo. "And you're getting all that from *this* photograph?"

A key rattled the lock, and Cleo whipped out her alarmingly large gun. I shook my head and pointed toward the back door. She dropped the spoon on the counter. I snagged Billy's picture off the table and escaped behind her.

A few minutes later we were back in the Camry staring down Jay Pruitt's front door.

"They're drug dealers." Cleo checked her gun. "Pruitt's going down."

"This is recon, chica. We observe from a distance. If he's a dealer, we pass it on. I have a cousin in the drug unit."

"Of course you do. So, what's your point?"

"No blazing guns, girlfriend."

"Yeah, right. Hold your breath on that one." She glanced at her watch. "You know, we're missing lunch. You're gonna wish you would have had some of that chicken casserole."

"I think I will be okay with missing out on that."

At 12:15 Jay Pruitt exited his house and drove off in a cream-colored Audi. He cut across Bridgeport and pulled to the curb smack in front of The Bridgeport Café.

"Holy crap," I squeaked.

Cleo parked across the street. I hunched low in my seat, peering over the dash. If my ex saw me, he'd be convinced I was stalking him. Again. He couldn't comprehend I could possibly get over his lying, cheating ass before the ink dried on the divorce papers.

Pruitt took a call on his cell before climbing out of the Audi and walking south on Morgan. He ducked into a building down the block.

"He's in," Cleo said smugly. "Drug deal going down."

I rolled my eyes. "That's the dry cleaners. He's picking up Linda's clothes."

"Uhm….you'd better sit up, Cat."

"I'm hiding from Johnnie Rizzo."

"Tall, dark, and oozing hotness?"

"That's Johnnie, dammit."

"Could he be wearing a shirt that says, *Here's Johnnie!*"

"What do you think?"

"I think he's coming this way."

I groaned and sank deeper. I cudda kissed the floor board.

Knuckles rapped on my window.

"He's here, isn't he?"

"Uh huh."

I jerked my head up, clonking my head on the dash.

Johnnie made a twirly motion with his hand. I unrolled the window.

"Ouch," I said holding my head.

Cleo flashed a tin badge. I'd swear she got it from cereal box.

"I'm Cleo Jones with Pants On Fire, narcotics division. Step back from the car, Mr. Rizzo. You're blowing our cover."

He made a little derisive scoff. "Right."

I jabbed an eye. "Another contact bites the dust."

"You have twenty-twenty vision. You don't wear contacts," he said.

"You don't know what I wear."

He searched my eyes and grunted, satisfied there wasn't a lone contact in there.

"You got to get over me, babe. Counseling, medication, something. You're pathetic."

Johnnie stomped off back to the café as I dropped my forehead on the dash.

"Argggh!"

"Damn girl, he's way hotter before he talks," Cleo said patting my back. "But then, men usually are."

Chapter Thirty-one

Jay Pruitt strolled toward us with a hefty armload of dry cleaning. We buried our faces in a map of Disney World. When he started up the Audi and merged into traffic, we did the same.

He drove north on Halsted and turned on Archer toward China Town. Traffic was moderate and we hung back, allowing a couple cars to bumper between us.

This stretch of Bridgeport has a long row of businesses and industrial buildings. The Audi slowed and swung left into a parking lot where two one-story gray buildings had been converted to storage units. The outside units were fitted with large garage-type doors. Pruitt drove to the gate and punched in a code. The gate opened, and the Audi drove inside.

Cleo drove past the entrance and pulled into the lot next door. The building appeared to be between tenants and showed signs of spotty, short term use. Cleo backed the car out of sight against the building.

We slipped out of the car and ran to the chain-link fence that surrounded the storage building.

"Wait here while I check it out," I whispered.

"Wow. Really? You know that's never gonna happen," Cleo said.

"Alright, fine. Just keep up and keep quiet," I snapped.

We walked along the chain fence, and found a spot under the security cameras that we could climb over without that whole pesky breaking and entering evidence caught on tape. I took off my jacket, threw it over the barbed wire. I hoisted a leg and climbed the chain fence, careful to not rattle the metal. I jumped down the other side and turned around. Cleo was gone. A moment later she trotted back with a pair of bolt cutters.

She waited for a noisy semi to come by. She clipped half a dozen links in the fence, stooped low, and scooted through.

"You know, you could have told me you had those before I ruined my jacket." I whispered over my shoulder as we zigzagged our way through the storage area.

"It's okay." Cleo whispered back. "I never liked that jacket anyway."

Pruitt was parked at a storage unit on the farthest side of the first gray building. The location offered maximum privacy. I wondered if that unit came by request or assigned by chance.

We moved swiftly and quietly across the lot, hugging the shadows when we could. When we reached the first building, we kept close to the front of the building. A dozen steps from the far corner we picked up muddled voices. A stench of cigarettes wafted through the air.

Pruitt's voice was easy to distinguish. Loud, heavily laced with testosterone. His companion was quieter, more thoughtful. It was the voice on the phone I couldn't place. I still couldn't.

I motioned for Cleo to stand back. Her ever-evolving hair was platinum blond that day with bold rainbow streaks that made a child in Jewel cry. Slowly, carefully, I craned my neck and poked an eye around the corner.

Pruitt leaned his back against his car, pinching a cigarette in one hand. He held a small object in the other hand. I couldn't make it out. But when he turned it a certain way, the sun flashed a glint of silver and blue. And when he smiled, a gold streak shot from his tooth.

His companion's back was turned to me. Head lowered. Jacket hood pulled over his head. No view of his face from that angle.

"When you comin' back?" the guy asked Pruitt.

"Four weeks, maybe five. Gonna let things cool."

The guy in the hat grunted. "My ear on the force tells me they got nothin'."

"That's good news."

"Gonna see your folks?"

"For a few days. Dad's birthday, ya know."

"Get him something from me. And you better check in on my mom."

"Dude, I always do. Besides, she'd kick my ass if I didn't."

Cleo whispered shrilly in my ear. "They're brothers."

I shook my head. "Cousins."

The ogre-guy dropped the shiny object into the other guy's hand. "See what you can do with this."

He nodded. "I'll get in touch with you when the coach thing blows over. Go on a trip to Hawaii or somethin'."

Coach thing? I couldn't breathe.

Pruitt said, "Why don't you head out too? The guys can look after things here."

He dropped his smoke and smothered it with his shoe. "Like grandpa used to say. 'Ain't no rest for the wicked.'"

They snuffed their smokes and stepped inside the storage unit. I had no view from my angle. I motioned to Cleo and we zipped back to the Camry, too stunned to speak.

"They killed Billy," Cleo said finally.

"We don't know that. The "coach" reference could be anything."

"I'm going with the big fat "Coach" sign on Rocco's uniform. Only Billy's killer would call him that."

I didn't argue. "We should talk to Captain Bob. He might have enough for a warrant."

"I'm hangin' with the car. The last time I walked in that precinct, Bob arrested me."

"Hate to break it to you, but he's not exactly crazy about me either."

"Of course he is. You're a DeLuca. He named his son after your dad. The ninth would shut down if the DeLucas went on strike. He was at your baptism for Godsake."

"People change, Cleo. Today he'd happily drown me with that holy water."

We moved the car to the other side of the gray storage building where I had a view of the keypad that opened the gate. When the cream colored Audi appeared, I lifted my binoculars and caught the code that opened the gate.

Cleo shot over to the ninth precinct and parked on the street. I strolled inside and poked a head into Captain Bob's office.

He groaned.

I said, "I thought you should know there's a second suspect in Billy Bonham's murder."

"Was there a first?"

"Kyle Tierney," I said. "The Irish Pub guy."

"Oh yes. My men are beating a confession out of him down the hall in interview room one."

I ignored the jab. "The man's name is Jay Pruitt. He's built like an ogre. And he has a gold tooth in the front."

"Why?"

"Many people underestimate the importance of flossing, Bob."

His face twitched. "*Why* do you think this guy is connected to Bonham's homicide? And who the hell is he?"

"Pruitt lives with the strip poker women. Billy's Christopher necklace was in their house."

"What was Pruitt's explanation when he gave you the necklace."

"Uh, he didn't."

"You *broke* into his house? You *stole* the necklace?" Captain Bob's voice rose with every word.

"*Seriously*, Bob. Can you really steal something that doesn't belong to that person?"

He searched my face, counting felonies like freckles.

I said, "I think Pruitt saw Billy in Rocco's coaching uniform. It had to be *after* I dropped Billy off at his mother's. Mrs. Bonham says he only went out once to walk the dog."

Captain Bob's brow shot up in surprise. "And Jay Pruitt told you this?"

"I uh, kind of overheard the conversation."

His brow lost some height. "You were stalking him."

"I'm a professional, dammit."

Bob took a bottle from his desk tossed back a swig.

"There's something else," I said. "Jay Pruitt owns a .32 magnum. The same type of gun that killed Billy. It wouldn't hurt to check it out."

"Who was this Pruitt talking to when he made the 'coach' comment?"

I shrugged. "I only saw the back of a head. There wasn't a lot of hair. But the comment should be enough to get a search warrant. Coming from a trusted source, that is."

"And you're saying someone was with you?"

"Ha ha."

"Caterina. I'm retiring next year. The missus wants to go on a cruise."

"Fab idea. You should go."

"The last time I listened to you, I almost lost my pension."

"C'mon Bob. That wasn't my fault." I stomped my foot for extra emphasis.

"No pension, no cruise." He shrugged. "Caterina, last spring you were hit by an exploding building."

"It was a vacancy sign."

"Well it took." He tapped his temple with an index finger. "Scrambled eggs."

"C'mon, Bob. I'm bringing you something good here. Run with it and you'll wow the big boys upstairs."

"You know what's funny about retiring?"

"Impending senility?"

"I don't give a shit about the guys upstairs anymore. My paygrade has peaked. My rank has peaked. I'm playing out my time. I don't want trouble."

He took a swill and pushed the bottle my way. I knocked it back and slammed it down on the table.

"Then be a hero to Mrs. Bonham. I'm a professional. I'm bringing you good intel."

"The last time you said that, I was almost reassigned to traffic duty."

"This is different. This is something you can sink your teeth into."

"People who lose their retirement don't need teeth. They live on baked beans and Spam."

He looked me over sharply until I felt the need to confess something. Sadly nothing juicy came to mind. When you're thirty and single, that in itself is a crime.

"Go away, Caterina. You have given me a headache."

I blew an exasperated sigh. "Last chance, Bob. Are you gonna check out this gold-toothed ogre or not?"

He pushed up from his desk and nudged me to the door. "I'll send you a postcard from Belize."

Cleo was sitting on the Camry's hood when I walked back to the car. She saw the expression on my face and winced.

"Did Captain Bob drown you with holy water?"

"He wanted to waterboard me. Luckily there were other DeLucas in the building."

"Did you ask him to get a warrant?"

"Of course. He's picking himself laughing off the floor about now." I blew a sigh. "We need to get inside that storage locker."

"C'mon, I have to show you something." She jumped off the hood, scooted around and opened the trunk. I stared at a black duffle bag.

"You should make me a partner. I got something Inga doesn't."

"An insane number of weapons for one human being?"

"Tools of the trade, girlfriend."

She unzipped the bag and removed the items one by one.

Hook and pick set. Handcuffs. An ankle knife and sheath. Rope, tape, latex gloves. Flashlights. Eighteen inch wrecking bar.

Ninja grappling hook. Tazor. Mace. Blow gun, a skull crashing baton.

"Geesh," I said. "A blow torch?"

"Too much?" She shrugged. "Someday we might need a confession."

"Take this." She gave me the knife and ankle sheath. "You never know when you're gonna run out of bullets."

"I'll use it to cut an apple."

Cleo tossed me the key. "You drive. You know where you're going."

I slid behind the wheel with a bad feeling about the storage unit. The kind of feeling you get when you know you're doing something stupid. I wracked my brain, but I was fresh out of smart.

"Where to, girlfriend?"

"Straight to hell," I said. "But I refuse to go there hungry."

Cleo nodded. "When taking down dealers, you can work up an appetite."

Twenty minutes later, we were in the heart of China Town at the Triple Crown. We ordered the dim sum and then I rang Mama.

For once, Mama believed the caller ID. "My precious Caterina!" she said.

"Gee, Mama. The last time you called me that, was when I told you I was getting married."

"It's good you remember how to make me happy."

"That happiness didn't end so well for me."

"Next time will be different." She laughed giddily. "I just got off the phone with Father Timothy."

Mama was up to something. Something she wasn't telling me. I almost asked her, but then I decided to be pissed off later.

"I'm wondering if you can keep Inga again tonight? I may be working late."

"What's to ask? She has her own little pillow and she sleeps between Papa and my legs."

"And that's okay with Papa?"

"Who do you think bought the pillow?"

"It's not natural to laugh when you talk about your priest," I told Cleo after I hung up. "Father Timothy isn't that much fun."

"Your mother seems to think so."

"That's cuz she keeps him entertained by confessing all my indiscretions."

"My mother hasn't been to church in twenty years. Trust me. If she thought she could confess my sins, she'd never miss a service."

It was mid-afternoon when we left the Triple Crown. We motored back to the self-storage building, changed our license plates a block away, pulled up to the gate, and entered the code. The gate opened and we cruised inside.

"Betcha we got a drug lab here," Cleo said.

We drove around to the far side where we eavesdropped on Pruitt and Co. earlier.

"This is it," I said braking at the second door down. "This is the storage locker. Okay, where is my floppy hat?"

"Here it is! I am putting together my own little box of tricks." Cleo pulled two identical hats from a box in the backseat.

"Zebra striped? This so doesn't match my outfit."

The large garage-type door was secured with a padlock that opened easily with a key. Or a lock and pick with an extra twist or two. We stepped outside, pulled out the latex gloves, and Voila! The lock was off.

Cleo's a bit of a drama queen. "Drumroll please." She swept a hand over her head and down to the ground. Her fingers gripped the handle.

"Jay Pruitt's drug business exposed," she announced.

The door lifted and Cleo gave a disapproving snort. There was, in a word, furniture.

"Crap," she said. "This is the wrong door. We should open a couple more."

I shook my head. "It's the one."

"But—this is, you know, just stuff."

I walked around, Actually, it was just *nice* stuff. This antique Tuscan coffee table. The Howard Miller grandfather clock.

I said, "There's a lot of money in here."

"So he's the ebay king."

"Maybe he does auctions. It could explain how he's in and out every time I break in his house."

"Annoying, isn't it."

Cleo snooped through drawers and a steamer trunk for a hidden meth lab or a couple Columbian drug lords setting up shop.

She stomped a foot. "Dammit. He was supposed to be a drug dealer."

"Admit it, girlfriend. You suck at codes."

I browsed around and one piece caught my eye. I picked up a mermaid. It was about eight inches tall and it was, in a word, magnificent. I checked out the bottom. It's signed by the artist. "I'd love to buy this."

"You'll have to leave him a note the next time you break into his house."

Tires scratched the gravel parking lot.

Cleo reached for the door. "Gotta run," she said.

I gave the unit a final sweep and my eyes froze on the smallest surveillance camera, high in the right corner.

Smile. We're on candid camera.

"Coming?" Cleo pulled me out the door.

We locked up fast, zipped around back, and drove up to the gate. A young couple in a U-Haul truck waved.

I didn't tell Cleo about the camera. I figured with nothing missing, fingers crossed, they'd have no reason to run the tape.

We cruised home without a lot to say. Cleo was annoyed that Pruitt probably wasn't the bad-ass drug dealer she made him out to be. My head hurt. The aspirin had worn off, but the bump behind my hideous bangs hadn't. My pocket felt warm where the photo of Billy was. A picture of someone stalking Billy stalking someone. We private dicks and janes are a surly lot.

I parked the Camry in front of my house and turned off the engine.

"Comin' in?" I asked. "I'll make tea."

"No thanks. I got stuff to do."

She grinned ear to ear and opened her coat. She pulled out the Vincenzo Bertolotti ceramic of a mermaid resting in a shell and slapped it in my hands.

"From Billy," she said.

I groaned. "You *stole* this?"

"They owe it to Billy. They took his brand new Chicago Bears jacket. Besides, there's so much stuff in there they won't notice."

"Trust me, they'll notice."

"Let them." Cleo grinned even wider. "They can't possibly know we were there, can they?"

I felt like I was gonna be sick.

I went inside and made ginger tea. The house was lonely without Inga to talk to.

I took my tea and the *Bridgeport News* into the living room. I put the Vincenzo Bertolotti ceramic on the mantle and sat across from it in the recliner. I might as well enjoy it. I'd have to return it tonight.

I sipped the ginger tea and checked out the Bridgeport social calendar news. The Italian American Club was having a Veteran's Memorial Brick Program. The Moose Club Fish Fry on Friday was not to be missed. The Catholic Church is having their annual Bingo-a-thon and bake sale. You know Mama will be there. Last year she won fifty dollars. She's a high roller now. She's been talking about taking a trip to Vegas ever since.

I skimmed down the page and Rocco's name caught my eye. Some dirt-bag reporter wrote a piece on a recent string of burglaries. The journalist slammed Rocco and Jackson. She dubbed them the Dubious Duo.

The article was totally bogus. The guys had been working their bums off on this case, interviewing victims, searching for a common denominator. The bandit was clever. He didn't leave a fingerprint or DNA behind. He'd mess up sooner or later. Until then, the ninth precinct was taking heat. And this commentary would not be lost on the brass upstairs.

For an added cherry on the throwing pie assault, an editor's blurb reported the Bridgeport Bandit struck again last night.

I called Rocco.

He skipped the *Yo.* "You saw the article," he said.

"It's crap."

"The guy's an asshat. He struck again last night."

"What did he take?"

"The usual. Jewelry. A laptop, still in the box. Some mermaid laying in a shell. Flat-screen TV."

"*What?*"

"What— what?"

I laughed. "You'd better come over, bro. You're gonna blow Captain Bob's socks off."

"Yeah?"

"I think the mermaid's on my mantle."

"Five minutes later the back door bell rang.

"How'd you get here so fast?" I said swinging the door wide.

Jay Pruitt stared at me. He had company. It was the Fence outside in the car at Devin's party. The bald guy with the voice I couldn't remember. It was all coming back to me now. And I sure as hell remembered something else. Freddy the Fence is a creepy, scary guy.

Jay said, "Can we come in?"

"No!" I tried to slam the door shut, but he had a foot in it.

Freddy said, "She's expecting someone."

His mouth twisted and the gold tooth glittered. "Whoever it is, they are gonna have to wait for a long, long time."

"ROCCO!" I screamed, knowing he couldn't hear.

I fought with all that was in me. I delivered a couple good punches and kicks that I knew I would pay for later. One jerked my hair back. The other duct-taped my mouth. Then he struck me in the back of my head, between the bottom of my ear and spine.

Everything went black.

Chapter Thirty-two

I woke in a dark place that smelled like funeral flowers. Hundreds of fragrance spewing, oxygen sucking funeral flowers. I wondered if I was dead. I tried to pinch myself, but my hands were tied behind me. My feet were bound and my chest strapped to a chair. I wasn't dead. I was pissed. And I was in the garden of hell.

I was pretty sure I could hear rats. The pattering of their little filthy feet, coming to climb up my legs and feast on my eyes. The sound got louder and faster. I couldn't breathe. My breaths came in short desperate snivels. I nearly blacked out again before I realized I was listening to my heart.

I did a mental head-smack. Willing my nostrils to take slooow, deeeep snivels. Captain Bob always said I piss people off. Jack, my smart-ass mechanic, said people wanted to kill me. Okay. So they were both right.

What do they want? A freaking cookie?

I decided if I get through this alive, I'm going to run that half-marathon with Max. I'm going to take Grandma DeLuca to a gypsy circus—even if it's in Italy. And I'm going to make arrangements to be cremated. Cuz if my big mouth kills me on any other day, I want my ashes thrown at Bob and Jack.

Planning my future—or even pretending I had one—helped me pull it together. First I would have to find a way out of here. Then I'd go home and have a meltdown with Ben, Jerry, and Captain Morgan.

I stretched low to the side, twisted my legs, and grappled Cleo's knife from my ankle. I breathed a thanks to the yoga gods and opened the blade.

On the upside, Rocco knew I was in trouble. He'd be looking for me. Every DeLuca in Chicago and every ninth precinct cop would come for me. I just had to stay alive until they figured out where I was.

A door shot open. Light from the doorway threw a long, ogre-like shadow at my feet. Creepy.

"You're back. Good. I told Freddy not to hit you so hard."

Pruitt was framed by flowers. Rows and rows of blue and yellow and red blossoms on the other side of the door. I was held hostage at a nursery. If I made it out, I'd bring Mama a big colorful bouquet. If I didn't, she'd buy flowers for my funeral. My heart beat pounded in my head.

Pruitt hit a switch and I scrunched my eyes, adjusting to the light. I looked around. Okay. No rats.

The room was painted pink and gray. The chairs screamed seventies. There was a large desk with drawers on one side and a door on the other. My friend Melanie's parents had one just like it. When we were kids, we'd climb through the door and hide in the desk. I saw piles of green tissue paper, baby's breath, gift cards, scissors, and tape on a table used for wrapping flowers. And I saw my 9mm Glock.

He pulled a chair up beside me. All cozy, like we were friends. Then he ripped the duct tape from my face. It hurt like hell. My eyes stung, but I didn't flinch. I wouldn't give him the satisfaction.

"Tough girl, eh?"

He hunched beside me, the big, meaty, red face sincere. "I'm Jay."

He was going for the Stockholm syndrome, where the kidnapped victim identifies with the kidnapper. Yeah right.

I said, "I know who you are. You're a thief."

"Am I?"

"Bridgeport Bandit. You've made quite a name for yourself."

"You think you're smart."

I shrugged. "Cleo thought you were a drug dealer."

His eyes darkened. "You've been a very busy girl, Ms. DeLuca. Sniffing around places you have no business. My house. My storage unit. Will Peterson's house. I need to know why."

"You should have given me the St. Christopher necklace, Jay. Mrs. Bonham only wanted to bury it with Billy."

"I told you I didn't have it."

"It was upstairs in a ballerina music box. Billy has it now."

His jaw tightened. It was obvious his roommates were supposed to get rid of it.

"Gee," I said. "Did I get someone in trouble?"

I kept him talking and worked the blade behind my back.

"I understand you were Bonham's partner."

I nodded. The only person he could have learned that from was the Prada woman at Billy's Wake.

"I'm going to ask you a few questions. I need you to answer them."

"Why?"

"Because the sooner we're done here, the sooner you can go home."

"Would that be in a box?"

"So cynical. I'm not a monster."

"Why did you kill him?" I said.

At first I thought he wasn't going to answer me. But then he thought, why not? The dead don't talk.

He said, "Will Peterson drove and I made the hit."

Keep him talking.

"How do you know Will?"

"I worked at his dealership. Before me and Freddie went into business together. A couple months ago we run into each other. Will's wife is gonna leave him. She's a greedy bitch. She'll ream him. He wants to stage a robbery. The thing with your partner wasn't personal. It was business."

"Not personal?" I choked.

"Your partner knew too much. It was an unfortunate necessity."

"Billy didn't know crap."

"Bonham was working for the insurance company. He photographed Will and me splitting the insurance money. He was gathering evidence. We didn't have a choice. We would have gone to prison for insurance fraud."

"You dumb-ass. The insurance company didn't hire Billy. Will's wife did. She wanted Bill to get her dog back."

Jay Pruitt was big and dumb and at a loss for words. He looked stunned, like I hit him. "I'll be damned."

Freddy's boxy square body walked in the room. "My guys are picking your girlfriend up."

"So what happens now?"

Freddy gave a twisted smile. "You know too much. You and Ms. Jones will argue, a lovers' quarrel, if you will. You'll kill her and then yourself."

"*Seriously?* That's the best you can do? No one will believe it."

"Forensics will prove otherwise."

"Think of my family. I'd rather die in an accident. I'll go over a cliff. I think you owe it to me a little dignity."

"There are no cliffs in Chicago."

"I'll go over a curb."

A car approached. Pruitt crossed over to the window and shoved the dark curtain aside.

"Your friend is here. It would be a good time to make peace with God."

Chapter Thirty-three

My hands were free. I sliced the rope around my chest and feet and exploded out of the chair.

The window opened easily. I threw the ropes outside as if I'd shed them running away. My 9mm was on the table begging me to shoot someone. I picked it up. It was still loaded. Then I opened the door on the left side of the desk. Twisting and bending in places God never intended, I slinked inside and closed the door. I peered through the keyhole and aimed my gun at the door.

Who's the human pretzel now?

I picked up voices and snatches of conversation through the open window. They were deciding where the fatal lover's quarrel would take place. My curb idea wasn't even on the table.

Freddy wanted to finish us up in the greenhouse and move the bodies. The greenhouse has cement floors and a hose. Somebody said they'd pick up bleach.

"It's risky to move a body and stage a suicide," Pruitt said. "They always catch those guys on CSI."

Cleo shrieked. "You're dead. All of you. D-E-A-D! When Frankie DeLuca hears what you've done, he'll chop you up in little pieces and feed you to the fish."

Pruitt laughed. "Let's go see your friend."

He tromped through the door, Cleo slung over his shoulder. She kicked and pummeled his back. His eyes cut sharply to the empty chair, and he almost dropped her.

206 K. J. Larsen

"What the—Shit! She's gone!"

Freddy raced inside, swearing viciously. "Find her."

"The gun. She took the Goddam gun."

There was shouting, and the car peeled away in hot pursuit.

There were just two of them again. Pruitt and Freddy the Fence. I could take them both out before they knew what hit them. If only Cleo would step out of the way. It was too risky to have guns blazing with her smack in the middle.

Cleo gave a hard laugh and shouted at the window. "You go, girl!"

Freddy's lip snarled. He whacked the back of her head with the butt of his Smith & Wesson.

Her knees buckled and before she hit the floor, a deafening howl—like the wail of a rabid animal—sliced the air. Frankie soared through the open window with a reckless bravado that would have done the FBI proud. Before Freddy's fumbling fingers could regrip the gun, he was pinned to the floor.

A thundering of footsteps followed. Rocco and Jackson led the Bridgeport Brigade in a charge through the door. Papa, the twins, Michael and Vinnie, Uncle Rudy, Tommy, and Leo were all hot on their heels behind, guns blazing.

Freddy's men had found Cleo. But Rocco got to her first. He knew they would come after her. And when they did he followed them.

"Where's my daughter?" Papa shouted.

Pruitt's voice sneered. "She's gone, old man."

Jackson pulled Papa off him and Rocco delivered a blow that should've knocked him to his knees. The ogre had already been hit in the head too many times. He shook it off.

I took a quick breath and prepared to sail out of that cupboard. Ready to unpretzel myself to the sheer amazement of all. When I tried to push open the door, my arms were tangled in a knot. I couldn't move. Anything. And my nose itched.

"Help! I'm here!"

My chest was crunched and my sorry whimper was lost in the sickening sound of pummeling flesh and a head bashing the floor.

I heard Max and Tino arrive, and they went straight to the twins.

"Where is she?" Max demanded.

"Gone," Michael choked. Vinnie stifled a small sob.

Max and Tino leaped onto the pile hammering Pruitt.

"Hello!" I croaked.

My pistol hand was asleep. Everything cramped and ached with an intensity I wouldn't have thought possible. I tried rocking. Pushing myself frontward and back, nudging a little further with each rock, until the barrel of my gun goaded the door open. I spilled forward.

"A little help here," I said and fell on my face.

Chapter Thirty-four

The hostess gave us a table by the window. It was where I confronted Tierney the other day. Before beefy-boy slung me over his shoulder and hauled me away like a sack of potatoes.

Good times.

"Can I start you with something to drink?"

I nodded to Savino, and he selected a bottle of California red from the wine list.

I said, "And would you tell Tierney that Cat would like to speak with him?"

"Cat?"

"Thank you. He's expecting me."

Kyle Tierney appeared shortly with a limited French private reserve label and three glasses. He'd soon regret the upgrade.

"We can take care of this in my office," he said.

"This is fine. I prefer witnesses."

He shrugged. "As you wish."

"Kyle Tierney, this is Chance Savino from the FBI."

Chance flashed his badge.

Tierney's ice blue eyes didn't flicker.

I pulled a napkin from my purse, unwrapped it, and placed Marilyn's diamond earrings on the table. His pupils got big. I thought he was going to kiss me. He kissed the diamonds instead.

He cradled the ice in his hands. "How did you find them?"

An image flashed in my head. Mitchell's honking huge Adams apple. And me rolling up the Philip Marlowe coat sleeves.

"Billy helped me," I said.

"For Godsake, Cat, I didn't kill your friend."

"Yeah. I know."

"You know?"

"My bad."

"Was that an apology?"

"It's almost enough to make me feel bad for what I'm going to say next."

"Which is?"

"I kept my word, Kyle. I brought you the earrings. Now I need them back."

"You're not serious."

"I'm returning them to Marilyn's estate."

"Why?"

I shrugged. "Cuz it's the right thing to do."

I placed my recorder on the table with the conversation my gold cigarette lighter caught in Tierney's car. I pushed play.

I said, "This is you kidnapping us. And admitting your part in the *Some Like It Hot* diamond theft."

Tierney cut the air with his hand. "I've heard enough."

I stopped the tape.

He sneered. "And you couldn't come here and talk to me without your FBI boyfriend behind you?"

Savino's voice was ice. "No one speaks for Cat, Mr. Tierney. I'm here for Cristina McTigue."

"Does Crissy know you're speaking for her?"

"No. I'm here to inform you that I intend to ask the FBI and the San Francisco County authorities to put Cristina on their watch list. If you hunt her down or threaten her, the FBI's Chicago office will be notified. If she's harmed in any way, if she's hit by a bus or chokes on a peanut butter sandwich, I'll know. I'll hand this tape over to the prosecutor and charges will be brought against you. You will go to prison. Do you understand?"

He shrugged. "Whatever."

"Cat is arranging transportation for Cristina and her daughter to return home to California. They'll leave in the next few days."

Tierney swallowed a smile. "Maybe a little sooner than that."

We followed his gaze out the window. A black Lexus sedan rolled to the curb. It had been washed and spit-shined since I saw it in front of the Marco Polo Hotel.

Cristina climbed out and danced around to the curb.

He stood saying, "Excuse me."

Savino held out a hand saying, "The studio is sending out a courier for the diamonds tomorrow."

Kyle pulled the earrings from his pocket and dropped them in Savino's hand. He gave a crooked smile.

"Can't blame a guy for trying."

Tierney walked outside and Cristina ran to him and threw her arms around him. He held her a long moment and said something in her ear that made her laugh. Then he let her go. She stood on her toes and kissed his mouth.

Halah sat in the car jamming to the radio. Close to her pepper spray. She gave Tierney a thumbs-up.

"Awesomity!" her lips said.

Cristina scooted over to say good bye to her friends. I gulped my wine, squeezed my eyes shut, and opened them again. I hadn't imagined it.

"Did you see that," I demanded. "*Unbelievable.*"

Savino shrugged and looked at his menu. "What's good?"

"Order for me." I scooted outside and joined Tierney on the sidewalk.

"You gave her your car," I said incredulously.

"It's a long walk to California."

"So why was she afraid of you?"

"Mitchell is dead. I did four years in an eight by twelve box cuz she got greedy. She figured I'd want payback."

"You were never going to hurt her."

"No. I wanted my share of the money. I figured she was living high all these years."

"And then you heard she was staying at the Marco Polo."

"That's when I decided she still had the earrings."

"You sent your meatheads after her."

"They were supposed to bring her back to the bar. I wanted to talk to her." He smiled. "And I wanted the earrings."

I winced. "I'll talk to my Uncle Joey about the meatheads. He knows how to make charges disappear."

He nodded. "Most appreciated."

Tierney was watching Cristina say good bye to her friends. She waved like Marilyn. She had the diva thing down. With or without the moola.

I said, "I'm sorry about pouring the whiskey on your head. And the whole thinking you killed Billy thing."

Tierney nodded slowly. "That was a hundred dollar bottle."

"You're still a schmuck."

He laughed.

"So are you going to tell me what really happened that night?"

"I met Mitchell before the heist. I liked him. He could make things disappear. But that night he was different. Nervous. I watched him make the switch. I said, 'Put both pair on the table.' I pulled my gun for a little encouragement. I wasn't going to knock him off or anything."

"What happened?"

"Crissy jumped me and grabbed the gun. It went off. We heard the cops."

"She ran to save herself."

He shook his head. "I told her to hide in the cupboard." He smiled—like Max had—and his eyes glazed over. "She's—"

"A human pretzel." I rolled my eyes. "I get it already."

Cristina hugged her friends and pranced around to the driver door. She blew Tierney a kiss.

"Love you," she mouthed and slid behind the wheel.

His ice-blue eyes thawed around the edges.

I didn't get it. Men dissolve to mush around Cristina. And she throws them under the bus. They buy her cars. They fall down dead. They go to the big house.

"Why didn't you tell the cops the truth?" I said.

"And face more charges? Fraud? Extortion? Burglary? I would have served more years in this state if they could have opened up that landslide than going down for this one charge."

The black Lexus sedan pulled from the curb and merged with traffic. He watched it drive away.

"And," he smiled softly, "I suppose I was in love with her."

"Really? Wow."

I turned around and glanced through the pub window. The cobalt blues held my eyes. My heart drummed in my chest.

"Good night, Kyle. I think my date is eating my supper."

I strolled to the door, stopped short, and wheeled back around.

"So you never would have chased Cristina to California anyway."

"No."

"And all that posturing back there. Savino flashing his FBI credentials. Me blackmailing you with the tape I made in the car. It was all for nothing?"

He shrugged.

I fixed my gaze like Bogie. I said, "But I was convincing, wasn't I? Even a little scary."

Kyle Tierney walked over and opened the door for me. The frost all melted from his eyes.

"You were...cute."

Chapter Thirty-five

I slipped back to the table, and Chance poured my wine.

I stared at the glass. "Can you believe that? After all she put him through, I think he's still in love with her."

"Probably."

"I had Tierney figured out all wrong. That's a pricey car. He just *gave* it to her. He's letting her go. That could be the greatest love of all."

Savino sipped his wine. "The Lexus has a tracking system, babe. By giving her the car, he knows *exactly* where she is. Always."

My eyes widened. "Ohhh. Duh."

The waiter brought our salads and crunchy loaf of sourdough bread.

"Maybe she's in love with him. I mean Cristina's a pain in the ass and Tierney's a schmuck. It could be destiny." I popped a tomato in my mouth and chewed thoughtfully. "Who knows? After all these years, they may find a happy ending."

The bartender brought a bottle of champagne to the table. He popped the cork, and the bubbles danced in our glasses. It was a Dom Pérignon. The good stuff.

"From Tierney?" I asked.

"From the gentleman," the bartender said with a nod toward Chance.

Oops. "I'm sorry. I thought—"

"It's okay, DeLucky." Chance smiled.

I closed my eyes and willed myself to slow down. It had been a tough week. I realized I was racing inside, still chasing ghosts and bandits.

I opened my eyes and looked at the bottle in the ice bucket. That was a chunky bit of change on a G-man's budget.

For an awful moment, I wondered if I'd forgotten something. Savino's birthday? Our four month anniversary? Chance seemed better at those things than me. I suspected there was a glitch in my genes.

I held the champagne to my face and let the bubbles tickle my nose.

"What's the occasion?"

He touched his glass to mine. "You are." He expelled an unsteady breath. "I could have lost you today, DeLucky."

The bubbles tickled my throat and a deep sense of happiness warmed me. I scooted my chair nearer, and we looked out the window and watched Bridgeport go by.

Savino leaned close and murmured something in my ear.

I smiled up at him. "What?"

He filled my glass again and watched me swallow every last sparkle of happiness before answering.

"Mom and Dad are coming next week."

I choked on a bubble. "Nooo!"

"They want to meet you. And your parents."

"I'm an orphan," I gasped.

Savino laughed. "Our mothers spoke this morning. We're on for dinner. Your mama's choosing a restaurant."

I groaned. "She's never known a vegan. She'll make reservations at a steak house."

"Your priest is joining us."

A strangled sound came from my mouth. I grabbed his glass and slugged down his champagne.

He laughed, enjoying this too much. "You'll be fine. It's just one night."

"From hell." I seized his collar and my voice squeaked. "You gotta call it off, Savino. Papa will try to get you to sign the Family Bible. Mama's bringing Father Timothy to book the church."

He put a finger to my lips. "Sshhh. Our parents aren't here."

He had a point.

He said, "I'm working on our own happy ending."

We finished the evening with cheesecake and a glass of Pernod. We drove home in Savino's big 1959 Eldorado boat car. Mrs. Pickins' binoculars followed us walking hand in hand to the door. He leaned down, and I put my hands on his face. He lightly touched his lips to mine.

I pulled him inside. "Mmm. Let's go to bed."

His eyes softened. "There's something I want you to wear tonight."

He pulled a box from under his coat. It was silver with hot pink ribbons and a bow.

I shook the box. It was light as air.

"Mmm. Lingerie," I said.

"Put it on. Surprise me."

I took the box into the bedroom. I stripped and pulled off the ribbon. There was a lot of tissue. And more tissue. And finally, there sparkled Marilyn's diamond earrings.

I slipped the earrings on my ears and looked in the mirror. I thought they made my boobs look bigger. I shook my hair down and walked into the living room.

Savino's voice was thick. "They take my breath away."

He wasn't looking at the diamonds.

To receive a free catalog of Poisoned Pen Press titles, please contact us in one of the following ways:

Phone: 1-800-421-3976
Facsimile: 1-480-949-1707
Email: info@poisonedpenpress.com
Website: www.poisonedpenpress.com

Poisoned Pen Press
6962 E. First Ave. Ste 103
Scottsdale, AZ 85251